Three indian
GODDESSES

...

Also by
JAMILA GAVIN

Three Indian Princesses

THE SURYA TRILOGY:
The Wheel of Surya
The Eye of the Horse
The Track of the Wind

Coram Boy
The Hideaway
The Singing Bowls
The Wormholers

For younger readers

Fine Feathered Friend
Forbidden Memories
Grandpa Chatterji
Grandpa's Indian Summer
I Want to be an Angel
Kamla and Kate
Someone's Watching, Someone's Waiting

Short Stories

The Magic Orange Tree

Three indian GODDESSES

...

By the winner of the
Whitbread Children's Book Award

JAMILA GAVIN

*The Stories of
Kali, Sita/Lakshmi and Durga*

EGMONT

The Girl Who Rode on a Lion
First published in Great Britain in 1993 by Ginn and Company Ltd

Copyright © Jamila Gavin 1993

Monkey in the Stars
First published in Great Britain in 1998 by Mammoth
an imprint of Egmont Children's Books Limited

Copyright © Jamila Gavin 1998

The Temple by the Sea
First published in Great Britain in 1995 by Ginn and Company Ltd

Copyright © Jamila Gavin 1995

This collection first published 2001 by Egmont Books Limited
239 Kensington High Street, London W8 6SA

Collection copyright © 2001 Jamila Gavin

Illustrations copyright © 2001 David Dean

The moral rights of the author and illustrator have been asserted.

ISBN 0 7497 4618 1

10 9 8 7 6 5 4 3 2

A CIP catalogue record for this title is available from the British Library

Typeset by Dorchester Typesetting, Dorset

Printed and bound by Cox & Wyman Ltd, Reading, Berkshire

Contents

To my children
Rohan and Indi

The Temple by the Sea

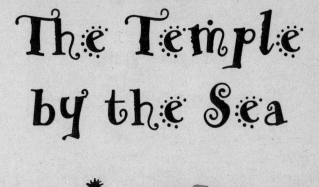

The Story of Kali

Chapter One

The Lonely Temple

THERE IS AN EMPTY STRETCH OF coastline which runs like a bleak lonely thread alongside the Indian Ocean. No one seems to go there, except for a few brave fishermen in their shallow open boats which are no more than one or two logs tied together. Each morning they risk their lives taking their nets far, far out to cast into the dangerous seas. Each evening they return with their catch – sometimes so meagre it could hardly feed a family – and plunge into the treacherous waves to drag their craft ashore before the great curtain of night closes on the sun.

Behind the coast, the fringe of jungle is still quite thick, although not much of it is left now; for behind it, the farmers have cleared the earth, carving out more space to grow crops. They have

2

no time for looking at the sea. Life is too hard. All day long they toil, guiding the plough, sowing the seed, watering the soil and then reaping the crop.

But once a year, they all turn their faces to the sea. Once a year they build a huge effigy of the goddess Kali, moulded out of clay and held together with sticks and straw. She is painted black, with fearful, wide, blood-shot eyes and a great tongue, which hangs out of her mouth dripping blood. The priests dress her in a glittering saree and drape her in pearls and precious stones. Then, with loud banging of drums, clashing of bells and the heart-piercing shriek of reed pipes, they parade their effigy through the village, across the fields and down to the old ruined temple by the sea, to unite her with her husband – Lord Shiva.

No one knows how old the temple is. It has been there throughout all memory and before. Its great granite edifice rises up like a chariot. Every inch of the hard grey stone is carved as finely and delicately as lace, with figures that leap and dance and work and play and love and die. It has wide terraces all around, with arches and columns

3

carefully designed so that the rising sun appears exactly through the middle at dawn, and sets in perfect symmetry on the other side.

It was here on these very stones, people claim, that Lord Shiva danced his dance of the Cosmos. And it was here that over the centuries, pilgrims, especially dancers, had travelled from all over India to pay homage to the great Lord Shiva. They would worship before the Destroyer of Evil, whose dancing feet crushed demons and whose whirling arms annihilated his enemies. The rhythm of Lord Shiva's dance is the heart-beat of the universe, and the pilgrims hoped that if they too danced on those same stones, the cosmic power would come up through the soles of their feet and they would dance like gods.

Then there was an earthquake – not in living memory, but over two hundred years ago. Some said Shiva got angry – but others insisted that it was his wife, the goddess Kali. They said she had become jealous of those dancers who had come to steal some of Lord Shiva's cosmic power.

Whatever the reason, some force had dragged the temple right into the waves – so that now,

even to this day, it is half in and half out of the sea.

From then on, a terrible legend grew around the temple. It was said that if any dancer came to dance on those ancient sacred stones, she would be cursed. It was said that the earthquake had released all the sorrows of the world; that the pain of all the souls of those who had died in torment would pass through into the feet of the dancer. Although that dancer would now dance as wonderfully as Lord Shiva himself, it would only last for a while – and then either the pain would drive the dancer mad, or she would wish she could have her feet chopped off to relieve the agony.

At first, the dancers still kept coming. There was always someone who laughed at the legend or thought it would be worth the chance of being the best dancer in the world – thought it would be worth risking Kali's displeasure to gain Lord Shiva's divine gift.

It was said that the Keeper of the Temple was grief-stricken at the loss of so many talented dancers. And he was terrified that one day Kali would again show her anger and try to destroy what was left of their precious temple. So he made

a secret pact with the great goddess. It is said that one evening before sunset, he stepped on to the accursed terrace and walked down its ruined slope into the sea. He tied himself to a half-submerged pillar to stop himself being swept away and all through the night he prayed.

The priests on the shore were certain they would never see him alive again. They saw the giant waves curling around him like serpents and they heard the voices of the drowned, gurgling up from the depths and shrieking into the wind.

All night long, the priests chanted hymns as loudly as they could to give the keeper courage. When finally the dawn light came spreading across the eastern sky, they walked silently through the ruins to the edge of the sea. They had expected to retrieve his body, but instead, they found that the keeper had untied himself and was walking back towards the temple. His face was serene and seemed to glow with a strange secret.

'It is done,' was all he would say.

Chapter Two

The Dream

FAR AWAY OVER THE OCEAN FROM THE temple by the sea, far away in England, lived a girl called Shanta.

The day Shanta decided she wanted to be a dancer was on her cousin Rani Shankar's thirteenth birthday.

A lavish party had been organised, for Rani's parents doted on their daughter. They were convinced she was the most beautiful and talented girl in the world – and that, soon, she would be known as the greatest dancer of her time. How they enjoyed showing her off.

Being extremely wealthy, the Shankars never did anything by halves. They lived in a large house, drove large cars, sent their children to the most expensive schools, and paid anything that

was necessary to ensure that their only daughter, Rani, had the best teachers and musicians to instruct her in music and dance.

But though they were rich, they were very generous and loved to have their house full of people. They loved celebrations and often threw parties — it didn't matter whether it was for birthdays or anniversaries, Diwali or even Christmas.

Rani's birthday was always considered a very special occasion. People looked forward to it, because everyone came, from the youngest to the oldest. Cousins and aunts and uncles and grannies and grandpas, and all Rani's friends from school — they all came. There would be mountains of food and rivers of wine and fruit juices; and a constant caravan of dishes would parade through with all sorts of savouries and titbits and delicious sweets. Although the Shankars always brought in the finest entertainers to amuse their many party guests, it was Rani herself who would be the star performer, rounding off the evening with a brilliant demonstration of her dancing.

Ever since Rani's birthday invitation had

8

arrived, Shanta's mother, Mrs Biswas, had been
fretting about what to wear. Mrs Biswas often
wore an expression of annoyance. She was mostly
annoyed because she felt her parents had made her
marry beneath her. Mr Biswas was a teacher and
would never be rich – not like Mr Shankar, Rani's
father, who was in business. Mrs Biswas envied the
Shankars' large house and big cars; and she
especially envied the beautiful sarees Mr Shankar
brought back for his wife whenever he went off on
a business trip.

However, every party invitation was received
eagerly – for it would be terrible not to be
included on the Shankar party list, even though it
meant terrible anxiety about what to wear. Mrs
Biswas dreaded looking poorer than the rest. She
would flick through the sarees which hung in her
wardrobe and then conclude in a very loud voice,
for the benefit of her husband, 'I have nothing to
wear. I'll just have to go shopping.'

'Why can't you wear that one of Banarasi silk
which I bought you on our last visit to India?'
asked Shanta's father in a pained voice.

'Because I wore that at the Mahajans' party, and

everyone would remember it,' retorted his wife, who could never be seen at a party in the same saree twice.

'I think you should wear that beautiful turquoise blue one with the peacock border,' murmured Shanta.

'Don't be silly, child,' pouted her mother, annoyed. 'That's not good enough for a party at the Shankars'.' She looked at her daughter and couldn't help showing her irritation. The girl was so awkward, so nondescript; so unpretty. Shanta's mother had never forgotten overhearing one of her sisters-in-law making the comment that if one must have daughters, at least they should be pretty.

'It's too bad,' Shanta's mother often groaned. 'Why should the Shankars have wealth as well as beauty?' She thought of her niece, Rani, with her fair skin, slender figure and face like a goddess, and compared her to Shanta. In her opinion, Shanta's skin was too dark, her forehead too broad, her feet too big and her figure rather stumpy. True, she had large glowing eyes, and people said of Shanta that her eyes and her rich black hair were

her most beautiful features; but where would eyes get you in this world? Who would want to marry her? Shanta's mother gave a discontented sigh. 'I suppose we had better decide what you are going to wear, too,' she said to her daughter.

'I shall wear the salvar kameez which Dad brought me back from India,' said Shanta. 'It's really lovely.'

The day of the party came round. That morning, when Shanta woke up, she felt a strange excitement stirring in her. She wondered why. She had been to parties before, so why, this time, did she feel a curious tightening in her chest — a kind of nervous excitement, as if something extraordinary was going to happen?

She got out of bed and looked in the mirror. It wasn't *her* birthday, but she felt different. She examined herself. No — there was the same old face and the same old body on the outside. Yet inside, her blood was racing and her feet were tingling. She stamped a dancer's stamp and twisted her hands as a dancer does. Her heart was beating fast like a tabla drum and she thought she heard a voice inside her head murmuring the dancer's

11

rhythm, 'Thakka-dhimi-thakka-jhanu-thakka-dhimi-thakka-jhanu!'

Then she remembered her dream. She had dreamt she was dancing in a strange temple. As she danced, she noticed that the stone walls were carved with figures of dancers. Their limbs twisted and flowed like the branches of trees, yet their torsos were as solid as the rock into which they were carved. You could almost hear the ankle bells jingling as they stamped their feet, and the rattle of tablas from the stone musicians who sat in attendance.

Suddenly, in her dream, the dancers came alive and leapt out of the rock. They surrounded her, urging her to dance too. But then the dream turned into a nightmare, for as the dance ended, she felt herself being drawn back into the rock with them and her body turned to stone. When she woke up and thought about it, she wondered if it was worth being turned to stone by day, if by night you could come alive and dance. For Shanta longed to dance more than anything. How she wished she was more like Rani.

Chapter Three

The Mysterious Tabla Player

WHEN THEY ARRIVED AT THE PARTY, Shanta's mother and father were immediately swept away into a glittering crowd of grown-ups. Rani's mother told Shanta to go and play with the other children out in the garden.

Was Rani out there too, Shanta wondered? Although Rani was three years older than her, they had become friends when Shanta had come to stay with the Shankars one summer, while her parents went back to India on a visit. The two girls liked doing the same things: they both loved dressing up and acting and dancing. They used to take it in turns to drum and sing while the other danced. They learned all the stories about Lord Krishna and the milkmaids and how he used to tease them,

and how he really loved Radha, the most beautiful of all the milkmaids. Sometimes Rani and Shanta danced before their family and friends, and this was how Rani's parents decided their daughter was really talented and should go and have proper dancing lessons. When Shanta begged her mother and father to let her go too, there always seemed to be an excuse. First she was too young, then the lessons were too expensive, then there wasn't really time – and anyway, she wasn't beautiful and talented like Rani, so it would be better to concentrate on something else. So Shanta, who had a cassette player in her room, used to content herself by dancing secretly to her music tapes and pretending that she was one of those dancers she saw from time to time in Hindi films.

At last Shanta saw her cousin at the far end of the crowded room. She wasn't outside playing with the other children, she was helping her mother to be a hostess, by passing round plates of samosas and taking away empty glasses to fill them up again. Shanta wanted to rush over and say hello – but suddenly she felt shy. Rani no longer looked like a child. She seemed to have grown taller since

they last met. She was wearing the most elegant salvar kameez of palest blue and silver. Her face was made up delicately, with powder and lipstick and a flush of rouge on her cheeks, and her eyes were outlined with black. Between her eyebrows was a simple red tilak and her black hair was gathered up into one plait and strewn with pearls. She looked so grown up.

Sadly, Shanta stepped through the French windows on to a smooth lawn. She could see the other children; they pranced about at the other end of the garden, confident, noisy and challenging, and she didn't feel like joining them. Somewhere, she thought she could hear the beat of a tabla. It seemed to be coming from an upstairs window so, when no one was looking, she slipped back inside the house and climbed the stairs, following the sound to the second floor.

The drumming grew louder; its beat was like a magnet and drew her closer and closer to it. Suddenly she found herself standing outside a door. How she could dare to open it she did not know, but as if in a dream, her hand took the knob and silently turned it. The door opened. The

drumming rushed out loudly, so she hurriedly stepped into the room and shut the door behind her.

The curtains were drawn and the room was darkened. A heavy rich smell of incense filled her nostrils and she saw the drummer seated cross-legged in a far corner with a pair of tablas, one under each hand. He had his back to her as he played, facing a small altar, in the centre of which was a dark iron statue of a god in a dancing pose. At first she thought it was Lord Shiva, Lord of the Dance; but then she saw the necklace of severed heads, the whirling axe, the tongue hanging out and a ferocious tiger leaping behind, and she knew it was the goddess Kali, dancing on the bodies of demons.

On one side of the goddess was an incense stick, its tip glowing red in the darkness and a thin coil of grey scented smoke rising to the ceiling. On the other side was a shallow saucer in which burned a thin flame. Laid before the goddess was a half coconut and an offering of rice and spices.

Suddenly the drummer stopped playing.

16

Shanta froze, terrified. She felt like a spy. She would have turned and fled from the room, but she was rooted to the spot.

The drummer changed from his sitting position and knelt low before the altar with his hands clasped in prayer. He murmured some words, lifted the saucer with the flame and circled it several times in the air before the statue. Then he replaced the saucer, tipped water from a bronze jug into the palm of his hand and tossed it over the fearsome Kali. When he had murmured more prayers, he returned to his cross-legged position and began to play again. He never turned and saw Shanta so, as his drum beats hammered into the air, she quietly opened the door and made her escape, glad that she had not been seen or heard.

For a while, she wandered about, nibbling whatever took her fancy and playing with the little ones who rolled and tumbled among the party guests. Then she noticed that Rani had disappeared, and she heard someone say that she had gone to change into her dancing costume.

At last, everyone was told to gather in the living room, where lots of chairs, sofas and floor

cushions had been placed in a semi-circle. Everyone made themselves comfortable and waited, murmuring with expectation. Shanta settled herself into a window seat at the side, and suddenly felt that same tremor of excitement surge through her. It was a nervous excitement, almost as if she herself were about to perform in front of all these people. Her fingers and toes were tingling and her heart was hammering.

There was a burst of applause as the same tabla player whom Shanta had seen earlier entered the room. She heard an awed whisper. 'Why, look! That's Mohan Datt, the master tabla player.'

He was a short, dark man; thin, yet powerful. He had the face of a hawk soaring in flight – distant, yet watching with microscopic eye. He wore a pure white Indian shirt and white pyjamas, with a dark red shawl slung around his shoulders. Walking at his master's side was a young disciple, a boy about Shanta's age. The boy was blind, although it was not immediately apparent for he walked as though he hardly needed the hand on his elbow that lightly guided him. The master tabla player sat the boy down on a carpet before a

wooden, stringed, long-necked musical instrument
– a tanpura – which was for strumming very
quietly as a drone. The Master then turned and,
with clasped hands, bowed and greeted the
audience with a namaste. It was the first time
Shanta had seen the tabla player's face clearly – and
it made her feel uneasy. His eyes roved over all the
faces waiting expectantly before him, yet without
really seeing them – until he turned his eyes on
Shanta. Then he looked at her hard and long, and
seemed to give her an extra special namaste all to
herself. It was as though he recognised her. Shanta
shivered. Had he known, after all, that she had
entered his room while he was praying?

The sound of jingling ankle bells heralded
Rani's entrance. Everyone gasped when they saw
how magnificent she looked in her dancing costume
of scarlet and gold. They clapped and smiled with
enthusiasm as she greeted everyone with a
namaste, and bowed before the tabla player. He
bowed low in return, then sat cross-legged before
his drums, one under each hand. Rani took up her
position in the middle of the room and stood, still
as a statue, waiting till everyone was settled.

19

The blind boy plucked the strings of the tanpura and a low note, like bees humming, resonated round the room. The drummer struck the skin of the tabla with a hard flat finger. It was like a single heart beat. He struck it again and then he struck the other drum. Now he began to play a slow beat. Rani listened, motionless. Then she moved her eyes in rhythm, looking from one side to the other; she lifted her eyebrows as if she were thinking magical thoughts; without moving from the spot, her foot took up the rhythm and tapped with a beat while her shoulders undulated.

From the back of the room, Shanta watched. She was entranced. The rhythm made her soul shiver. Her eye caught the eye of the tabla player; he seemed to be beating the drum for her. Shanta slipped unnoticed out of her seat and, as if hypnotised, began to move with the beat.

At the front, Rani glowed like a sparkling flower. Her beauty dazzled, her movements were so graceful. Everyone's eyes were on her, smiling with pleasure, so they didn't see how Shanta danced. Shanta danced and danced, forgetting where she was, her ears only hearing the liquid

beat of the tabla and her body turning from that of a stumpy child into a gracefully moving figure, like a temple statue come to life. Her face was transformed so that she no longer looked like that little girl her mother thought so 'unpretty'. There was a look on her face as if she had glimpsed paradise – and it made her the most beautiful person in the room, if only anyone had bothered to look.

Rani entered the climax of her dance, whirling round faster and faster and faster with her long plait flying, her skirt spread out like a spinning top and the bells on her feet jingling like galloping horses. Then, with a joyful flourish, she came to a stop, her face flushed and beads of perspiration glistened on her skin.

'Wonderful! Brilliant! Exquisite!' There weren't enough adjectives to describe what people thought of Rani, but then a voice was whispering in Shanta's ear: 'You dance beautifully, my dear. I should like you to be my pupil.'

Chapter Four

The Chosen One

SHANTA'S FACE WAS FLUSHED WITH THE tremendous energy which had gripped her body and moved through her limbs. Her head was bowed when she heard the voice – an old, quavering, wrinkled voice, yet somehow harmonious, like a musical string. Shanta looked up slowly, her eye travelling from the floor, where sticking out from beneath the border of a saree, were a pair of thick boots. Up . . . up . . . her eyes travelled wonderingly. Up through the folds of the sari, and the drapes of a shawl until she found herself looking into the most ancient face she had ever seen, with skin as brown and creased as a walnut and with eyes as luminous and deep as moonlit waters.

'You are a dancer of the stone,' murmured the

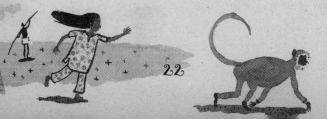

old woman. She put her hands on Shanta's shoulders and pressed her fingers into Shanta's flesh, feeling her muscles and sinews. She moved her hands up her neck and to her head, moving it this way and that as if testing its strength.

'Yes, you have a body that is solid and strong but which will flow like water. I can teach you to be the best dancer in the world.'

Shanta's brain was tumbling with thoughts. Somehow, she had known from the moment she had woken up that there was something different about this day. But how could she have known that today her entire future would be decided?

'Will you let me teach you?' asked the old lady, though her voice almost seemed to command it.

'I will . . . if my parents allow me.'

'They will. I'll see to that.' The old woman spoke with low confidence, and then moved away to be lost in the crowd.

'The old lady is Uma Rao!' Shanta's father spoke the name with awe and amazement. 'She was once known as the finest dancer in India. Then, at the peak of her powers, she disappeared and no one ever saw her dance again. Even the Shankars didn't

know who their lodger was until now.'

'Just think of it!' Shanta's mother exclaimed with glee as they drove home after the party. 'Uma Rao wants to teach *my* daughter. Not the fair, beautiful Rani Shankar, but *my* daughter, Shanta Biswas. Who would have thought that our dark little girl could be so special? Doesn't it just show you – money can't buy everything! Of course the old woman is very eccentric – I mean, did you notice she was wearing *boots*? I ask you. But the famous can afford to be eccentric, so who cares?' She turned to her daughter. 'You could be famous and become rich and look after us in our old age. So I hope you'll work hard and do everything Uma Rao tells you, even if she makes you dance in boots too. That was the deal. She doesn't want any money. She just wants your complete obedience and dedication. You'll have to make some sacrifices.'

Shanta smiled quietly. At that moment she felt she would have given the old lady her soul in exchange for being able to dance.

So it was arranged, just as the old lady promised. Each Friday after school, Shanta was to

24

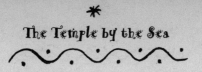

cross the city and go for a lesson with Uma Rao in her basement flat in the Shankars' house.

The first day, she met her cousin on the steps. 'Hello, Rani!' cried Shanta, so pleased to see her friend. But Rani did not return her smile. She looked strained and cold. 'I've come for a dancing lesson. Aren't you pleased for me? It's what I always wanted,' cried Shanta joyfully.

But Rani suddenly narrowed her eyes and spat out jealously, 'Don't let it go to your head. You'll never be a dancer. Look at you – you're not pretty; you're just a lump. You'll never be as good as me, you can't be – not even with Uma Rao as a teacher!' She flounced indoors.

Shanta felt her heart grow so heavy she thought she would choke. Had she just made the first sacrifice – her friendship with Rani? She wanted to run after her and say, 'Don't worry, Rani. I won't dance. I'd rather be your friend.' But then she saw the old woman beckoning to her through the basement window, and she obeyed the silent command to come in.

Shanta entered a bare room. There were no carpets to cover the wooden floor boards. There

were just a few cushions in one corner.

Uma Rao stood in the centre of the room. Her saree was drawn up and tucked in like loose trousers, which made her look even more bizarre in her boots. Yet she could never be a figure of fun. There was something about her too proud, too mysterious, too commanding for anyone to laugh. On the contrary, Shanta felt a tremor of anxiety as the sharp, needle-like gaze seemed to pierce her very thoughts.

The old lady bowed a formal namaste and Shanta did the same. Then the old lady took her behind a curtain and told her to change. She was to wear a pair of cotton, jodhpur-style trousers and a thin, close-fitting blouse, and there was a set of ankle bells for her to strap round each ankle. When Shanta emerged, tinkling with every step, she found that the blind boy who had played at the party was sitting on the cushions before a pair of tablas.

'Prem will play for you,' said Uma Rao. 'Although he is blind, his ears are better than most people's eyes. He will follow you and know your every mood and gesture just as if he could see.'

So the dance classes began.

Week after week, Shanta crossed the city by bus to go to the old lady's basement flat for her lessons. But though Prem was always there, they never spoke to each other. Uma Rao would not allow talk. 'Dance is the language of movement and expression,' she would say. 'We do not need speech.' They would not dare to disobey her. Uma Rao didn't need speech to show her displeasure. One look from her told you instantly of her anger or her satisfaction.

So Shanta never had a chance to chat to Prem, for he was always there before she arrived, and he left before she did, to go back to his master. He had been dedicated to Mohan Datt since early childhood. From then on Mohan Datt had been father, mother, teacher and guru to him. One day, Prem would be a master. He too would have a disciple, and in this way, the skills of tabla-playing would be passed on from one generation to the next. But while he was a pupil, like Shanta, he had to show total obedience.

The old lady was very strict. It wasn't just that Shanta had to learn to dance, she also had to learn

to pray and meditate. 'Dancing is the same as praying,' Uma Rao told her. Before every dancing lesson. Shanta had to sit cross-legged and concentrate. She had to learn to become the character she was dancing — whether it was a milkmaid or a goddess, a fish or a bird. Most of all, she had to dedicate herself body and soul to Lord Shiva. So, just as she had seen the tabla player kneeling before the altar, lighting incense sticks and murmuring prayers, Shanta did the same.

Week by week, month by month, Shanta got better and better. She knew it. She could feel it. She felt her body hardening up as her muscles strengthened; she felt her arms and fingers developing their own language, flowing more fluently than words from a mouth. As for her eyes… People who saw her dance said it was her eyes which made her special. They were so dark and deep; they could glow with love or flash with anger, they could quiver with expectation or drown with sorrow. Sometimes, to look into Shanta's eyes was like looking into the eyes of the Creator.

And wherever Shanta's mood and imagination

took her, Prem, the blind boy, was there too. Rhythms which mirrored and echoed her dancing feet bubbled out from under his thin bony fingers as they moved over the surface of the drums; and though Prem and Shanta never spoke, it was as though he had become a part of her and understood her completely.

Every now and then Shanta had that dream of dancers in the rock, who leapt out of the stone to whirl through the night and then returned again to their petrified form. One night, one of the dancers was Uma Rao. But in Shanta's dream, Uma Rao wasn't old. She was young and strong and as beautiful as a goddess. Yet there was something terrible about her. Although she danced more magnificently than any other dancer, her face was drenched with tears, and then Shanta saw that, instead of bare, stamping feet, Uma Rao danced in boots.

One day, Uma Rao left the room briefly. Shanta took a chance and dared to talk to Prem. She wanted to ask the one question which had become an obsession and burned in her brain.

'Tell me,' she whispered urgently and quickly.

'Why does the old lady wear boots?'

'Why?' The boy's voice hung in the air like a long spider's thread. 'I hope you'll never find out,' he murmured. He could say no more as the old woman returned.

Then, one day, the master tabla player, Mohan Datt, came into Shanta's lesson. He didn't play, but sat cross-legged on the floor next to Prem and watched her, as on the day when he had played at Rani's thirteenth birthday. For an hour, he sat rigid, not saying a word. Shanta was aware of that same intense gaze, focusing on her like some spotlight, which followed her round and would not release her from its hold.

'Is this the Chosen One?' he asked in a low voice.

'She is,' answered Uma Rao.

'Is she ready?'

'She is,' nodded the old woman.

Then he and Uma Rao had a whispered conversation together in a language that Shanta didn't understand.

When the tabla player left, Uma Rao took Shanta's hand and said, 'Shanta, the most

important thing has happened. Something that every dancer yearns for. You have been invited to dance at a temple in India. It is a temple by the sea. It is very holy, and only a few chosen dancers in every lifetime are asked to dance there. The call has come for you. You must obey.'

Shanta did not often look directly into her teacher's face except when she was learning a dance expression. Usually, her eyes were lowered with respect and she only spoke when spoken to. But there was something so strange in the way Uma Rao told her this news. The old lady's words told Shanta something which should make her the proudest and happiest girl in the world, yet there was a terrible sadness in Uma Rao's voice which made Shanta look wonderingly into her teacher's face.

'My dear . . .' said the old woman with unexpected tenderness. She stretched out a hand and gently touched Shanta's face. 'If only . . .' She stopped and, as if afraid, turned abruptly away. 'Get changed quickly.' Her voice was harsh. 'I will come home with you and tell your parents so that they can make plans immediately. I'll just get my shawl.'

Once more, Shanta and Prem were briefly alone. But this time, it was Prem who made the first move. 'So you are the Chosen One,' he murmured, leaping to her side. His agile fingers moved up her arms and shoulders feeling their shape, then travelled like spider's legs, fluttering across her face, feeling her nose, her mouth, her cheeks, her chin – taking in all her features through his fingertips. Then his thin fingers gripped her arm, hurting her. 'Listen to me,' he said urgently.

Shanta was startled and couldn't help stepping back from the boy who stared up at her with sightless eyes.

'What is it?' she cried. 'What's the matter?'

'The time has come. Now I must warn you. Please listen.' He spoke rapidly, his voice quivering with anxiety.

'What do you mean, warn me? Warn me of what?'

'You are a Chosen One. That means that Uma Rao has chosen you to be a dancer for the goddess Kali. Now that she has taught you everything she knows, my master has arranged for you to dance in

India in the temple by the sea. Only then will Uma Rao be freed from the curse. They will want you to dance on the terrace which the waves wash over when the tide comes in. But you must refuse. I warn you – refuse to dance there. For if you do, you will be cursed forever, just as the great Uma Rao was cursed.'

'What do you mean, cursed? How?' cried Shanta.

But before the boy could answer, Uma Rao had reappeared wrapped in her shawl, telling Shanta to come.

'Will Prem be my tabla player?' Shanta asked.

'Oh no!' answered the old lady. 'The master himself will play for you in the temple by the sea. But Prem will be there. A disciple is never apart from his master.'

Chapter Five

Leaving Home

'I DON'T WANT TO GO!' SHANTA remembered how she had forced those words from her lips, after Uma Rao had explained to her parents that she had been chosen to go and dance at the temple by the sea.

Her parents had reacted fiercely. 'What do you mean, you don't want to go? Of course you do, silly girl. Didn't you hear what your teacher said?'

Oh Yes, Shanta had heard the old lady's powerful words. 'Only the very best dancer in any generation is asked to dance there,' Uma Rao had said. 'It is the highest honour, for your feet will stamp on the very stones on which Lord Shiva danced. His power will surge through the soles of your feet and you will dance like a god.'

'Do I also dance for the goddess Kali?' Shanta

dared to whisper.

Uma Rao looked startled, briefly, as if a secret had been let out. Then she smiled stiffly and said, 'Kali too, of course. Is she not Lord Shiva's consort?'

But Shanta also remembered the urgent warning of the blind boy, Prem. She had looked at Uma Rao's boots and longed to ask the question that now burned in her brain day and night – 'Why do you wear boots? Is it to do with the curse?' But whenever she felt her courage rise and opened her mouth to ask, she would lose her nerve and sink back silent and angry with herself.

'You promised total dedication and obedience in exchange for dancing lessons,' her father reminded her. 'So if Uma Rao wants you to dance at this temple in India, then you must go – and that's an end of it,' he said sternly, seeing Shanta's mouth open again to protest.

Shanta stood in her bedroom. Her eyes roamed lovingly round its walls. Pictures which had been there since the day she was born still hung there – pictures into whose depths she had often wandered in her imagination.

She picked up her oldest and dearest toy – a stuffed monkey, which she had had since she was a baby. Its fur was almost worn away in places from the hugging and kissing she had given it over the years. She looked into its glassy eyes and murmured, 'I'm going to miss you.' For Uma Rao had told Shanta that as she was going to India, she must put the past away and say farewell to her childhood.

Shanta looked up and saw herself in her wardrobe mirror. Was she no longer a child? How often she had stood in front of that mirror and examined herself. How often she had critically sighed over what she thought was her ugliness. 'If only I could be as pretty as Rani,' she used to think, 'then perhaps Mum and Dad would love me more.' How often she used to watch herself dancing. 'When I grow up,' she used to whisper. 'When I grow up I want to be . . . I wish I could be a . . .' She would go right up to the mirror and press her face against her mirror image and whisper the word 'dancer'.

Ever since she became Uma Rao's pupil this greatest wish was no longer a secret. Everybody

knew that Shanta Biswas was going to be a dancer.
Now when she looked in the mirror and saw her
dark face and arms, she felt special. She no longer
wished she looked like Rani. Lord Shiva was dark;
the dark, blue-throated god who danced the dance
of creation.

Once when she had danced particularly well,
she thought she heard Uma Rao murmur, 'Yes . . .
yes! You are truly a child of Shiva!'

She treasured those words, for Uma Rao hardly
ever praised her – not like that. Usually, the most
she would say was, 'That's the way.' Those words
were enough, coming from someone who was so
critical; and anyway, Shanta soon didn't need to be
told when something had gone well. She could feel
it in her own bones and see it by the small smile
which would creep over Prem's face. Even though
the boy could not see her, he could tell by every
single other one of his senses; by the stamping of
her feet and the excitement of the sung rhythms
which echoed round the rooms from the voices of
Shanta and her teacher. 'Thakita-thakita-thakita-
dhim! Thakita-thakita-thakita-dhim!'

Now she could look in her mirror and say,

'When I grow up I *am* going to be a dancer.'

This was her last day in her own room. Tomorrow, she was going to India. She knew she should be feeling great happiness. Isn't this what she had always dreamed of? Yet she was full of foreboding. Prem's words haunted her and filled her with a deep dread. She had tried to believe that her dancing was all for the good. But Rani had stopped being her friend. Even though Shanta went over to the Shankar house once a week for her dancing lessons, Rani no longer invited her in as she used to. Sometimes Shanta longed for the old days when she and Rani were friends.

When Rani knew that Shanta was going to be a dancer, it had made her jealous and competitive. 'I'll show her!' she hissed spitefully. 'I'll show that plain, dumpy little cousin of mine she isn't a patch on me.' Rani had worked even harder at her dancing and was indeed becoming famous. She was often invited to give performances and had even danced on television.

But when Shanta told Rani that she was going to dance in India, in the temple by the sea, Rani had become rigid, as if her body had turned to

stone. 'It is you who should be going,' cried Shanta, painfully aware of her cousin's jealousy. 'I don't know why they chose me, when you are so beautiful and dance so wonderfully well.'

'Oh, but I *am* going!' Rani had suddenly burst out triumphantly. 'They have organised a tour of India for me, didn't you know? I'll be there too, don't you worry.'

Shanta didn't know and wasn't sure if it was true, but she smiled generously and said, 'Oh good!'

As the day of departure had drawn nearer, Shanta felt more and more disturbed. She had remembered Prem's warning. What had he meant by a curse? Shanta wished she could talk to him further and find out more, but she had never been left alone with him again, not for a single moment.

Suddenly, as she gazed at her mirror image, she thought she saw the room behind her open up into a fearful cave, where beyond, a great dark sea heaved and curled and looked as if it would hurl itself on top of her. She spun round, trembling with terror. The door flung open and her father came in.

39

'Shouldn't you be in bed, dearest?' he asked gently. 'We have a big journey ahead of us tomorrow.'

'Oh Dad!' She rushed into his arms and clung tightly. 'I don't want to go,' she whispered, and burst out sobbing.

'Hey, hey, hey! What is all this? What's got into you, Shanta? We're coming with you. This will be the most important dance of your life.'

'Please, Dad, don't make me go to India tomorrow. I don't want to dance at this temple. Prem says . . .'

'What's all this nonsense? What does Prem say?' Shanta's mother burst in. 'You don't want to go listening to that silly boy. After you have danced at the temple, you won't just have that sightless boy as your tabla player, you'll have the master himself. Now get to bed and get your beauty sleep.'

'Beauty sleep?' Shanta cried even more. Before she had become Uma Rao's pupil, no one had thought her beautiful, not even her parents. But now, because they had been told that she would be a famous dancer, they all called her beautiful.

40

Even more beautiful than Rani, they said.

Suddenly, she stopped crying. She dashed the tears from her eyes. Perhaps after all, this was part of her strange destiny and it would do no good to fight against it. 'I'm ready to sleep,' she said calmly, and firmly ushered her amazed parents from the room.

As Shanta lay in the darkness she stopped thinking about the future. She thought only of Prem. Dear blind Prem, who had never seen her; never judged whether her skin was too dark or her eyes too big or her body too stumpy. Somehow she felt no one else in the world really loved her as Prem did, and she was suddenly comforted. Whatever happened in India, at least Prem would be there – somewhere.

Chapter Six

The Night Before

A WIND SWISHED ACROSS THE SURFACE of the ocean like a scythe. It chipped into the sea sending up flurries of white foam, and hewed out deep troughs into which fishing boats vanished, then reappeared, poised, almost as if they would fly from the sharp-ridged crests of the waves.

The farmers straightened their backs, looked briefly out to sea and wondered if they were in for a storm. They did not envy their brothers, the fishermen, whose sails they could see dotted over a wide area, still far from the shore.

A priest stood in his saffron robe on the partly submerged terrace of the temple, holding a holy thread and sacred beads. He chanted prayers and tossed marigolds and bits of coconut into the rising tide. 'Soon, soon!'

He stretched out his arms. 'Soon, O Kali, we will offer you another dancer – the best we can find – to glorify your temple.' His words mingled with the screeching of the seagulls that wheeled and soared and pecked at the waves.

Back in the village, the people had been in a frenzy of preparations for the Kali Festival which had come round once more. Using sugar cane and bamboo and dried leaves, and moulding it all together with clay, they gradually built a huge black effigy of the goddess Kali.

This year, the priest had told them, was a special year – a propitious year. They would be offering another dancer to Kali to placate her anger and save them from any more earthquakes. So they had built their effigy of Kali even taller than usual, and the villagers had donated some of their finest cloth and jewellery to adorn this fearsome goddess. They placed the figure on a chariot and she towered twenty feet above them – suddenly seeming divine, even though they had made her with their own hands.

It was the night before the full moon. The

night before Shanta would dance at the temple by the sea. As the giant orange sun sank into the ocean, they raised an oil-filled lamp on to a high pole, and through the enveloping darkness, those fishermen not yet home fixed their eyes on the shining light and made for the shore. All around, glimmering from every household in the village, were oil-drenched wicks burning in honour of dead ancestors.

'Is she here?' the priest asked Mohan Datt. The two men stood among the walls of the temple, where the ocean heaved at their feet and the stone people crowded round them looking as if they would leap out of the rock and join in the festivities that throbbed through the darkness.

The master tabla player nodded. 'We have brought you the best. Tomorrow, here on the temple terrace at sunset, she will dance and we will offer her to Kali. Then Uma Rao will be free.'

In the shadows, the blind boy listened and his tears overflowed.

Shanta had never been to India before, yet she was told this was home. She stood at the window of the simple brick house on the edge of the village

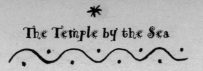
and gazed out across the brown tilled fields. The
bullock pulling the plough had followed the lie of
the land; it coiled in swirls among mango groves
and clumps of banana trees, and cut furrows which
ran right to the very edge of the sea.

A full moon was rising, and already there were
the sounds of pipes and drums and chanting
voices, and children squealing and laughing, and
garlands of bells jingling round the necks of
horses and bullocks. It seemed that every living
creature was intent on celebrating the Kali
Festival. People had made new clothes to wear,
decorated their houses, painted their animals,
threaded hundreds of garlands of flowers – so that
the air was cloying with the smell of marigolds
and jasmine and tube lilies. They had lit their
oil lamps and placed them on their roofs and
balconies and verandas, shining as bright as day.

Shanta could hear the excitement and
happiness all around her, yet she felt terribly
afraid. She could see Prem standing at the edge of
the field, his face turned into the wind which blew
in from the sea. She knew that he too was afraid. If
only she knew why.

She was alone in her room with instructions to pray and meditate in preparation for her dance at the temple. But she couldn't control her thoughts or her fears, though she tried over and over again, kneeling before an image of Shiva. She remembered that she had first glimpsed the master tabla player kneeling before Kali, not Shiva. To whom should she pray? She lit several incense sticks, trying to let the thin smoky smell invade her mind and help her to concentrate on her performance, but it was hopeless. Over and over again, she went to the window and looked out across the sea, wishing she was back home in her own room in England. Why, oh why had she ever wanted to dance?

A distant movement caught her eye. She saw Uma Rao taking a back path which led down to a lonely part of the shore. She had fresh clothes draped over her arm, so Shanta knew she was going to bathe. In an instant, Shanta realised that this was her only chance to satisfy her curiosity. Without any further thought, she slipped out of her room, across a back veranda and down on to the same path which led to the sea.

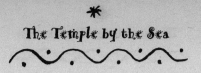

The Temple by the Sea

It was a gradual track which took the old lady gently down to the shore.

Moonlight and sunlight together glittered on the waves like gold and silver coins. Without removing her clothes, Uma Rao waded out into the sea. Then, when she was waist deep, she unwound her saree, took off her blouse and submerged herself completely, the loose cloth swirling around her. Then Shanta nearly cried out with terror and excitement. Uma Rao dipped under the water again and removed her boots. One by one, she tossed them onto the shore, then threw up her arms and began to chant prayers.

Shanta crept as near as she dared and hid behind a rock, just a few yards from where the old lady had placed her new dry clothes. She would have to come out and then, Shanta knew, this would be the moment when she would see the great dancer's feet at last.

Uma Rao's prayers seemed to go on for ever, then suddenly, they stopped. The old lady turned and seemed to look straight at her. Shanta recoiled out of sight, her heart almost leaping out of her chest with fear. Had she been seen? She heard faint

47

splashes, as Uma Rao waded ashore. Pressing her body into the curve of the rock, Shanta risked another peep. It only took one look. One dreadful look. She fell back, fainting, stuffing her hand into her mouth to stop her crying out. At last, she had seen what she had craved to see. She had seen Uma Rao's feet.

Chapter Seven

The Dance of the Temple

SHANTA'S MOTHER HELPED HER TO dress. The best tailor had stitched Shanta a magnificent dancing skirt and trousers in scarlet and gold silk. Her long black hair was plaited and coiled with jasmine and pearls, her eyes were outlined in black charcoal and her skin brushed with a pale powder which made her gleam. The palms of her hands and her feet were intricately patterned with henna and Shanta was bejewelled – she was spangled with jewels like the night sky. Clusters of pearl dangled from her ears; they were linked by a thin chain of gold to a glittering diamond stud which gleamed on her nose. Necklaces of emeralds and rubies entwined her throat and descended in a criss-cross of gold chains across her midriff. Gold and silver rings flashed on

her fingers and toes; the bracelets on her arms and the bells round her ankles tinkled with every movement.

'For goodness sake, girl, look a bit more cheerful. Your face is as glum as if you were going to a funeral. This is the most important day of your life,' her mother begged her. 'From now on, they will treat you like a goddess.'

But it was as if Shanta – the Self – had vacated her body and left an empty shell.

When she was finally led from the house, people thought Shanta was in a trance, for her face was as expressionless as a doll's. She was held by her father on one side and Mohan Datt, the tabla player, on the other, and they seemed almost to carry her along.

A fantastic procession had formed, with jogging musicians and excited families, decorated bullocks and finely groomed horses. They brought out the elephant from the temple – all painted and garlanded and carrying four or five young boys, who supported a tall effigy of a dancing Lord Shiva. Young, strong-muscled men with huge, fringed umbrellas ran alongside a chariot which

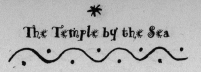

was completely entwined and draped with flowers. On top of the chariot, swaying as if she were alive, was the great black figure of Kali. If special disciples had been chosen to pull her along, you could hardly see them, for everyone wanted to help – men, women and children, the young and the old, the pregnant, the weak, the sick, the crippled and the blind. They all wanted to touch, to see, to just be within Kali's shadow so that some slight speck of her power might fall upon them and bring them good fortune.

They made a space for Shanta behind Kali's chariot. No one crowded round her. Instead, they fell back with awe, whispering and pointing, with a strange dread on their faces.

'Is she going to dance at the temple by the sea?' asked a child's high voice.

'Ssssh!' They dared not answer.

The temple seemed big enough to absorb everyone. They swarmed all over it; up the terraces, along the walls, among the ruins, up and down its many steps; some even into the sea itself, slithering and slipping on the seaweedy boulders.

But into the innermost sanctum, into the

darkest heart of the temple, they led Shanta. The only light came from a low sacred flame, tended by two saffron-clad priests, who softly chanted and tossed holy water and waved sticks of rich incense. The light flickered over two giant figures carved out of the rock.

Only then did Shanta seem to come alive. She turned to the figure on whom the dawn rays fell each morning. Her eyes travelled up its immense torso, till she found herself gazing at the most beautiful, powerful face she had ever seen. Lord Shiva gazed down at her out of the rock. Two eyes, though carved in stone, seemed to glimmer with a life force. The third eye, in the middle of his forehead, was half-closed, not wanting to look upon the faithful in case its power should destroy them.

'Oh please, Lord Shiva, save me!' Shanta sent up a silent prayer. 'I only wanted to dance – that's all. I don't want to be the best or the greatest. I don't want fame and fortune. I only want to dance to make me happy.' She would not turn and face the other figure, Kali, who was equally huge, whose fearsome shape seemed ready to leap out of

the rock and devour her.

The master tabla player nudged Shanta to approach the sacred fire. He took her hand and passed it three times through the flame, while prayers rose and echoed round the cave. Then a priest pressed his thumb into a mixture of ash and dung and vermilion and smeared it on to her forehead. He sprinkled holy water over her head and feet and then blessed her.

Uma Rao stood in the shadow of one of the columns, merging into it like a statue. The master tabla player left Shanta and sat before his tablas which had been placed on the terrace, whose stones were already being lapped by the incoming tide. The blind boy sat beside him, strumming the tanpura. Its note droned and reverberated as if awakening the souls of the dead. As Shanta walked out to take her position in the centre of the terrace, Prem lifted his face towards her as if seeing her with his blind eyes.

'Dance now. Dance, my child,' murmured Uma Rao. 'Dance with the spirit of Lord Shiva. Be our sacrifice. Dance to placate the anger of the goddess Kali. Dance to free me from the curse.'

53

The tabla began its beat. Shanta stamped a foot and picked up the rhythm. She caught the eye of the tabla player, just as she had done – was it a lifetime ago? – at Rani's birthday party. He seemed to hypnotise her, and she felt her whole body giving in to the need to dance and dance and dance.

'Ahhaaah!' She heard the ecstatic sighs around her as her magic began to work.

A wave rose up and fell on the terrace steps, part of it swirling towards her, but just receding before it touched her feet.

Prem's finger faltered on the strings and the hum of the drone was interrupted. But Shanta hardly noticed. She was dancing better than she had ever danced in her life and she never wanted to stop. 'Thakka-dhimi-thakka-jhanu, thakka-dhimi-thakka-jhanu!' The tabla player's voice rang out over the beat of the drums. Her feet stamped in answer, her eyes gleamed and flashed out their messages.

Another wave rose and fell. This time, only a step backwards saved Shanta's feet from being submerged. Prem laid aside the tanpura and stood

up. Everyone was in a trance. He heard the next
wave coming from far off. He felt it gathering
itself together, coiling up its head like a cobra,
poised and ready to dart out across the terrace. The
tabla player beat the drums even harder. Shanta
leapt towards the sea as if to embrace the wave and
at that moment, with a great cry, Prem threw
himself upon her and dragged her out of the
temple.

The drum beat hardly stopped for breath, for in
that instant, another dancer sprang into Shanta's
place on the terrace stones. 'Let me, let me dance!'
she cried. The tabla player nodded and smiled, as
Rani picked up the rhythms and gave herself body
and soul to the dance.

The wave had waited – as a cobra waits to
strike – but now it broke, and in its fall, it was as
if it released the piteous voices of a million
tormented souls. It swept across Rani's feet. Wave
after wave rose and fell, till soon the terrace was
submerged in the sea. But Rani danced on until
the waves lifted her from the ground and her feet
could stamp no more.

Epilogue

AFTER THE FATEFUL DAY AT THE TEMPLE, Rani Shankar became known as the most fabulous dancer in the whole world. Rani danced before the greatest – in all the grand theatres. She was adored, as no one else was adored – though just a few said that to see Shanta Biswas dance, accompanied by her blind tabla player, was to see a child of the gods.

Then one day, Rani disappeared. It was exactly ten years after she had danced in the temple by the sea. For a while, people were distraught and searched for her high and low. But then they forgot Rani, just as they had forgotten Uma Rao, and they turned instead to Shanta and wondered why they hadn't thought her the greatest all along.

More years went by, till one day Shanta went to a theatre, out of curiosity, to see a young dancer perform. It was said that this young girl was

destined to be the finest dancer of her generation.
As the child danced, Shanta noticed her teacher, a
woman, standing in the shadows of the stage,
watching intently. With a gasp, Shanta hurriedly
left her seat and made her way backstage. She was
sure she knew the teacher and wanted desperately
to talk to her. She rushed along dark corridors and
finally came up on the other side of the stage from
the woman.

As the marvellous child whirled about between
them in the spotlight, the two women met each
other's tragic gaze. Even from that distance, Shanta
saw the boots poking out from beneath the simple
saree. Then she knew. Her heart burst with pity as
she raised her eyes again and dared to look into
Rani's face. Slowly, Rani bent and took off her
boots. Shanta knew what she would see. It would be
the same as when she had spied Uma Rao coming
out of the ocean. For a moment, she turned away in
dread, but then, her eyes brimming with tears,
Shanta looked back to her cousin and childhood
friend and saw the feet of stone, the same hard,
grey, granite stone of the temple by the sea.

Shanta never saw her own teacher, Uma Rao,

ever again — at least not as a living human being. It was as though she had never existed. But one day, when Shanta was nearly old herself, she and Prem found themselves travelling near the village with its temple by the sea.

'Stay here, Prem, at the rest house and bathe,' Shanta said gently. 'I want to take a walk and stretch my legs after our long journey.'

Prem sighed. He knew where she was going, but he didn't try to stop her.

She wandered along a dusty track which ran between the rice fields and soon reached the lonely, grey, granite stones of the temple. The rise and fall of the waves and the calling gulls mingled with ghostly voices, vibrating strings and hammering drums. She touched the rock face, running her fingers over the carved figures of dancers who almost seemed to turn and watch her as she moved slowly past them.

Suddenly she stopped and stared. One figure caught her eye. It was a beautiful dancer sculpted out of one of the columns which held up the roof over the terrace, where Shanta had danced on that fateful day. A life-sized statue of a woman gazed

down on her, just a little taller than she was. The woman's feet were raised in a mighty stamp – Shanta could see all the toes spread out with energy – and so perfectly carved they could have been living feet. The arms were raised as if gracefully beckoning. Then Shanta looked into her face. Perhaps spray from the sea had been swept in by the wind and gathered in all the delicate ridges and lines of the sculpture; but as Shanta looked into the stone face of Uma Rao, she saw tears trickling slowly down those hard, grey cheeks.

Nearby, on the great stone frieze, behind Uma Rao and the line of dancers, was a space in the rock waiting to be filled.

Monkey in the Stars

The Story of Sita/Lakshmi

Chapter One

Monkey on the Wardrobe

'OW!' AMRITA SAT BOLT UPRIGHT, FULLY awake. Moonlight flooded into her room through the open window. There was a strange silence, broken from time to time by something cracking and crunching. She looked around trying to work out what the sound was and where it was coming from. Something hard and small rolled into her hand. She fingered it curiously, trying to identify it in the darkness. It was the size of a large pea pod, but ridged and brittle. She squeezed it and it cracked loudly.

A strange high voice piped from nowhere, 'That's an empty shell. Here have this.' A small object flew through the air and struck her on the nose.

'Ow!' Amrita switched on the light. 'Ow, ow,

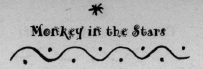

ow!' she squealed, as she was pelted by another and another. And then she saw the mess. Scattered on the sheets and all over the carpet were . . . monkey-nuts! 'Oh my goodness! What a mess!'

'Go on, open it, eat it, eat it! These peanuts are excellent,' came the voice again – a voice which hardly seemed human. It was crackly, chattery, ripply, giggly – and, as it spoke, a shower of empty peanut shells cascaded down from the top of the wardrobe.

'Hey!' protested Amrita, raising her arms to protect herself.

At first, all Amrita could see was a long, coiling, hairy, silver tail. Then, from within the depths of the shadows at the top of the wardrobe, she made out a curved body shining with silver fur, a round, black, leathery face, two mischievious eyes glinting from beneath furry eyebrows and a grinning mouth, inside which she could see a row of sharp, white, star-bright teeth.

'Here, have another!' A monkey-nut hurtled down. Amrita automatically caught it. 'Good catch!' trilled the creature.

'What are you?' Amrita finally gasped.

The creature leapt from the wardrobe, swung from the ceiling light and landed with a plop on her bed. 'What do you mean, what am I? Can't you see?' He wagged a black, bony, long-nailed finger at her. 'What's this?' He stroked his long fur. 'What's this?' He bounded on all four legs round the room. 'What's this?' He stood upright on two legs, getting taller and taller and taller till his ears brushed the ceiling. 'And what's this?' He looped up his great serpentine tail, which seemed to be growing longer and longer all the time. 'It's not possible that you don't know what I am.'

'You look like a monkey, but . . .' stammered Amrita, sliding down under the sheets, till only her eyes and the tip of her nose showed above the covers.

'Look like a monkey, indeed, but . . . but what?' snorted the creature.

'You're not any old monkey!' she finished weakly.

'How observant of you,' he scoffed. 'Of course I'm not just any old monkey.' He leapt from her bed and landed on the window ledge. Outlined in the moonlight, he looked silver and gold, animal and human, tiny but gigantic, light and

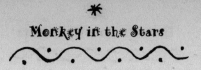
shade . . . he looked like . . .

'Hanuman!' Amrita whispered the name.

'Ah-ha!' the monkey breathed with satisfaction, and a light wind rippled all round the room, ruffling Amrita's hair, billowing the curtains and scattering the monkey-nut shells across the floor. 'Yessss!' he proclaimed, his voice suddenly sounded like distant rain.

'I am Hanuman, Lord of the Monkeys. I am the fighter against evil, the servant of Vishnu. I am of the past, present and the future.'

'Why . . . ?' Amrita struggled to form the simple question.

'Why am I here?' Hanuman asked it for her. 'Why am I here? Why am I there? Why am I anywhere?' he answered teasingly. He flicked his tail across the room. It fell in a blaze of sparks across her bed. 'Hold on to my tail, little Amrita. Come with me! Diwali, the Festival of Light, begins tomorrow. All over the world, the tailors have been at work, cutting and sewing new garments from woven cloth, and the dye-workers have cast the cloth into wonderful colours. Let's see if the walls of every home have been whitewashed

and the floors swept clean and decorated to welcome the Goddess Lakshmi. Let's see if evil has been driven from the universe. Let's see if Prince Rama has defeated the King of the Demons and rescued Princess Sita.'

Amrita jumped out of bed. 'Oh yes, let's!' She clasped the Monkey God's tail. She wound it round her like a sash. 'I'm ready!' she cried, flinging wide her window. With one bound, Hanuman leapt among the stars with Amrita safely entwined in his tail.

Chapter Two

Tricked by the Demon

PRINCESS SITA HUDDLED INTO THE OLD trunk of a banyan tree, whose twisting creepers hung like a cage around her. The demons danced and shrieked, circling her like a band of moths round a flame. Every now and then they thrust their long claw-like fingers through the leaves to pinch and poke at her.

'Oh, Rama, Rama!' she wept. 'Will I ever see you again? It's all my fault. Lakshmana was right – it was a trick.'

Sita lived in the jungle with her exiled husband, Prince Rama. His father wanted him to rule the Kingdom of Ayodhya, but his second queen wanted her son, Prince Bharata, to be king. Years ago, she had saved the king's life and, in return, he had granted her two wishes. For a long

time she did not use the wishes, but now she demanded that Rama should be banished to the jungle for fourteen years.

Everyone knew this was like a death sentence, for the jungle was full of wild animals and demons, and they were horrified when Sita said she would go with her husband. Prince Lakshmana, Rama's younger brother, asked for permission to go with them and, with a breaking heart, the old king agreed. So the three left the kingdom.

They had been in the forest for some time when Sita saw the most beautiful creature in the world — a deer, whose golden fur had patterns like shining moons and whose horns were twisted with silver and tipped with sapphires and diamonds. She longed to have its fur for a cloak. When she told Rama about it, he immediately grasped his bow and unsheathed his arrows, ready to hunt the deer.

Lakshmana warned him: 'Don't go, brother! Don't go. You know there are demons in the jungle, and this might be a trick.'

But Rama said, 'Look at Sita. She is a princess, yet she looks like a beggar. She has given up everything by joining me here and, until now, she

has never asked me for anything. How can I refuse
her this one request? I'm sure I will be all right,
but promise me, Lakshmana, protect my Sita while
I am away. Do not leave her alone – not for one
minute.'

Lakshmana promised, and Rama sped away, his
bow and arrow at the ready. But Rama didn't come
back. Then, from out of the jungle came a cry
which sent the parrots hurtling into the air.
'Lakshmana, Lakshmana! Oh, brother, help me!
My life is in danger! Come and save me! Quick,
before it's too late!'

Lakshmana and Sita clasped each other in
terror. Then Lakshmana grabbed his spear, and he
was about to rush into the jungle to save his
brother when he remembered his pledge never to
leave Sita alone. He stopped and fell to his knees.

Sita was bewildered, then angry. 'Lakshmana,
why do you hesitate? Are you afraid? Are you such
a coward that you don't go this instant to save my
husband?'

Lakshmana was in tears. 'How can I, Sita? I
promised Rama I would not leave you alone for
one single moment. How can I disobey him?'

Sita's anger was terrible. 'If you don't go and save my husband, I will never call you brother again. If you don't go, I will!'

Rama's terrified voice continued to plead. 'Help me, help me! Come quickly! Save me!'

Lakshmana took a piece of chalk and drew a circle all round the hut, chanting special prayers as he did so. 'Sita, I will go and search for Rama but, whatever you do, do not step outside this circle. It will protect you from all evil.' Then he left her all alone.

Hours went by, and neither Rama nor Lakshmana returned. The jungle sank into an unnatural silence and Sita was afraid.

The sun was almost out of sight beneath the trees, when she saw an old holy man. He came hobbling out of the forest looking frail and exhausted. She cried out joyfully at seeing another human being: 'Holy man, holy man! Are you hungry? Come, I have some food to give you.'

'Yes, my dear, I am hungry. I have walked all day, and my bowl is empty.'

Sita ran inside the hut and scooped up some food on to a banana leaf. She rushed out again and,

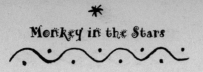

in her enthusiasm, almost stepped outside the circle. Just in time, as her toe touched the edge, she drew back. 'Holy man! Please come closer so that I can put this food into your bowl.'

The holy man stood rooted to the spot, his bowl still held out, just a few paces away but out of reach. His orange clothes seemed to burn like fire; his eyes glowed like coals. Yet, when he spoke, his voice was so gentle, so kind. 'My dear, you know I am not allowed to go to you and take, you must come to me and give.'

'But . . . I promised not to step outside the circle . . .'

The holy man shrugged sadly. 'It is up to you.' He turned away.

Sita told herself. 'He is a holy man and he is old. It is against God's law to allow a holy man to depart empty handed. Surely I have nothing to fear from him? He is so close. All I have to do is leap out and, in just two steps, give him the food and get back inside the circle.' So she called again. 'Holy man, stay, I will come to you.'

The holy man paused and turned as Sita stepped outside the circle. She took one step, two,

71

reached out, and put the food into the bowl.

Then something dreadful and terrifying and abominable happened. In one great flash of lightning, the gentle, sweet holy man grew and grew and grew, turning into a monstrous, ten-headed, twenty-armed demon, with twenty rolling bloodshot eyes. It was Ravana, King of the Demons.

Like a whirlpool, Sita was sucked into Ravana's arms. From out of the sky, he summoned his chariot, pulled by two-headed demon horses, their hooves spraying sparks. With a wild laugh, he flung Sita inside. How she struggled and screamed as Ravana whipped up the horses and they galloped away into the sky to his island of Lanka.

Ravana begged Sita to marry him. The voices from his ten throats hummed sweetly like honey bees: 'Forget Rama,' they sang. 'Come and live with me and be my queen, and I will give you all that your heart desires.' He played the veena to her, hoping he could enchant her with his music and make her love him.

Day after day he came to her, but each time Sita had cried, 'Go away! I shall never marry you.

Rama is my husband and he will be for ever.'

When at last Ravana realised that Sita would rather die than marry him, he flung her out of the palace and sent her to the wildest part of the garden to be taunted by his demons.

As Sita sat huddled under the banyan tree, it seemed to her that even the stars looked unkind and the moon uncaring.

But something was moving across the heavens, swirling and bounding, sweeping through the Milky Way and plummeting towards earth. A falling star? A plunging comet? The brightness came closer, heading straight for her. Sita buried her face in her hands, blinded and terrified.

It was Hanuman, with Amrita wound into his tail. Like a shooting star, he descended. He landed without a sound, yet the earth trembled on his impact, and a deep anger rushed through him. Amrita felt his whole body quake. 'What is it? What's wrong?' she stammered.

'Look at her! Look what they've done to the beautiful Princess Sita!' His whisper turned into a hiss of rage.

'Is that Princess Sita?' Amrita stared at the

73

weeping young woman. 'Wife of our beloved Lord Rama?'

Amrita looked through the darkness at the dancing lights which she thought were fireflies. Then she realised they were the devilish eyes of demons, who whirled around Sita. They pulled her long hair, and pinched her arms till they were black and blue. They clawed at her with long curling fingernails, and bared their blackened teeth as if they would bite chunks out of her. And all the time they jeered and spat, 'SSSSSita! SSSSStupid girl! TTThhhhinks she's too good to MMMMMarry our king! Worse than a SSSSSnake! LLLLower than a worm! We'll teach her. We'll teach her to know her place.'

Filled with pity and outrage, Amrita screamed, 'Stop it! Stop it! Stop it at once! Leave her alone, you bunch of bullies,' and she rushed among the screeching, taunting demons and threw her arms round Sita to protect her.

In a flash, Hanuman turned himself into a tiny monkey and leapt into the tree. Coiling his tail round an over-hanging branch, he hung upside down until his mouth was close to Sita's ear, and

he whispered sweetly, 'Take courage, dear Princess. Help is near. Rama is coming to rescue you. Be brave. It won't be long now.'

Sita raised her head in wonder. She looked at Amrita and then at Hanuman.

'Rama? Is Rama near? Does he know I'm here?'

'He will soon.'

'Grrrr . . .' screamed a demon. It leapt in with a pointy, poky finger and jabbed Sita. She winced with pain.

Amrita lashed out. 'Get away! Get away you horrible creature.'

Hanuman's anger rushed through him. It was so great, it made him grow and grow and grow. He grew bigger than the tree. He grew bigger than ten trees standing end to end. He was so angry, the moon and stars disappeared and the night sky became even darker.

'How dare you treat the Princess Sita like that,' he thundered and, in his temper, he ripped up trees by their roots and hurled them among the demons; he scooped up hundreds of squealing monsters and flung them aside; he rushed about like a tornado, stamping and trampling as many

of them as he could.

'Oh no, Hanuman! Stop, stop!' moaned Sita. 'Calm yourself. You cannot destroy the demons.'

Amrita saw this was true, for no matter how many demons Hanuman killed, thousands more rushed out. They swarmed all over him, and even though he was taller than a giant, they brought him crashing down.

'Hanuman!' Amrita whimpered with fear, as they dragged him away. 'What will they do to him?' she asked, turning to Sita. But Sita had fainted.

All through that night, Amrita and Sita heard the chanting: 'Kill, kill, kill! Kill, kill, kill!'

The demons had dragged Hanuman before Ravana, King of the Demons.

'What shall we do with him?' they shrieked. 'Shall we chop him up into little pieces?'

But Lord Ravana shook his ten heads and smiled ten evil, cunning smiles. His ten voices crooned like a flock of doves. 'No, no, no, no, no, no, no, no, no, no! Killing is too good for him. First we shall shame Hanuman – bring him down a peg. Then we shall use this snivelling, scrawny monkey as our messenger. Ha! What better way of

76

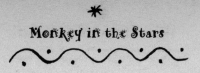

showing Rama that his powers are piffle in the wind compared to mine, and that he can do nothing to get back Sita?'

'Yesssss, yessss, yessss!' hissed the demons gleefully. 'But how shall we shame Hanuman?'

'What does Hanuman have that he treasures more than anything else?' demanded the King of the Demons.

The demons thought.

'Is it his silvery fur?'

'Is it his mighty strength?'

'Is it his wind-like speed?'

'No, no, no, no, no, no, no, no, no, NO!' roared Ravana.

'What then?' they asked running out of ideas.

'It is his TAIL, of course!' he bellowed. 'His tail, you idiots! Go get a fiery brand!'

Quick as a flash, several demons raced off and returned with a huge burning brand. The flames soared from it, brighter than the sun. The demons recoiled from the terrible heat and hid their eyes.

'Hanuman! I could kill you, but I won't. Let's see what kind of a monkey you are without a tail!'

The demons fell about, howling with laughter as Ravana took the brand and held it to Hanuman's long, shining tail.

There was the sound of sizzling and crackling and spitting. Hanuman's tail began to burn. Then a sheet of fire flared into the sky as the tip of Hanuman's tail burst into flames.

Amrita watched in horror. 'Why did you start a fight, Hanuman?' she wept. 'Why didn't you just go and get Rama?' She held Sita fearfully in her arms.

'Hee, hee, hee!' Amrita couldn't believe her ears. Hanuman was chuckling. He stood there with his tail on fire, laughing his head off while he became smaller and smaller and smaller. The demons tried to grab on to him, but only burnt their fingers or grasped at empty air. In a thrice, Hanuman had grown so small, they could see nothing except the glimmering fire of his tail. Like a glow worm, he slipped away.

Hanuman fled across the walls of the garden and on to the palace roofs, his tail burning like a meteor. But as he fled, he grew bigger again. He leapt from wall to wall and house to house setting

the whole city alight from end to end.

Long into the night, Amrita heard the demons screaming and scattering in panic, not knowing whether to save their city or themselves.

'Thank goodness,' Sita murmured with relief.

'He's got away.' The princess leant her head against Amrita's shoulder and slept for the very first time since Ravana had tricked her in the jungle.

I hope when Sita is rescued, I'll be rescued too, thought Amrita sinking into sleep herself.

Chapter Three

Amrita's New Clothes

'WAKE UP, WAKE UP, CHILD!' AMRITA'S granny was shaking her. 'Naughty girl! Look at the mess! Fancy eating monkey-nuts in bed. Get up now. You'll have to clean your room before we go shopping to buy you Diwali clothes.'

Amrita got the dustpan and brush and swept up the shells. As she did, she sang. 'It's true. It all really happened. But surely it's not over yet?' Then she remembered Sita, and sat back on her heels. 'How come I'm home? Poor Sita! She's all alone with those demons. I should have stayed until Rama came. Hanuman, where are you?'

She ran to the window wondering if she would catch a glimpse of the Monkey God – up the apple tree, on the fence, behind the dustbin, down the alleyway. She saw a gleam of fur and a tip of tail,

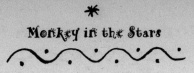

but it was only next door's cat.

'Come on, come on, come on!' her mother's voice urged her from downstairs. 'Granny's waiting for you. She wants to get going. Everyone will be out shopping today. Diwali is almost upon us – and I still have so much cooking to do for the party tomorrow.'

'Oh dear!' sighed Amrita. 'Everyone's going to be moody today.' She followed her grandmother out of the gate.

'Don't frown, child,' snapped Granny, 'otherwise you'll have grumpy wrinkles when you're old.' A deep furrow divided her eyebrows as she wagged her finger at Amrita. Then, hugging her shopping bag close to her body, Granny stumped off towards the town centre.

Amrita would usually have been hopping and skipping ahead, and her granny would have been calling out, 'Don't go so fast, child! Have pity on your poor old granny.' But, today, Amrita was trailing behind listlessly, and Granny was grumbling, 'Keep up, keep up! What's wrong with you, child?'

'Ow!' exclaimed Amrita, as she felt her

81

ponytail tugged hard. 'Stop it!' She whirled round expecting it to be Steven, the boy from a few doors along, who was always so annoying. But there was no one there.

A tickly puff of wind blew into one ear then into the other, making her squeal with laughter. But in the next breath she was shouting, 'Ow! That hurt!' as something trod on her toe. She hopped about. 'Ow! that hurt!' mimicked a whispery voice.

Then something tripped her up. 'Ow, ow, ow!' yelped Amrita. 'What are you doing? Stop it!'

'Stop it, stop it, stop it!' mimicked the voice sounding like Granny.

'That's no way to talk to your grandmother,' Granny stopped and turned round with a scowl. 'Are you making fun of me?' she asked suspiciously.

'I wasn't talking to you, Granny,' Amrita tried to explain.

'To whom then, may I ask? I see no one else. Do you make a habit of talking to trees or lampposts?'

'Oh, Granny, I thought . . .'

'And why are dawdling behind like this?'

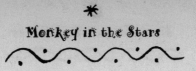

continued Granny without taking a breath. 'Don't you want a new Diwali dress?'

'Oh yes! I do!' Amrita tried to sound pleased, but she knew what kind of dress her grandmother would insist on buying her, and she felt ridiculous already. It would be the kind of dress she hated – shocking-pink and all frills, bobs and bows, and fancy stitching and smocking, and lace and layers of petticoats, which stuck out as if she was wearing an umbrella. She would have to wear matching pink socks and matching ribbons in her hair – and she'd look an idiot. Amrita sighed, then gave a wriggly scream as something which felt like a beetle dropped down the back of her T-shirt.

'Really, Amrita,' snapped Granny impatiently. 'Walk in front where I can see you. And stop all this nonsense!' She gazed with exasperation at her granddaughter leaping about, tearing at her clothes.

'Something's gone down my back. I'm sure it's a creepy-crawly!' Amrita bellowed. 'Get it out, get it out!'

Granny held her still and lifted up her T-shirt. 'Ha!' she snorted. 'That's what comes of eating

peanuts in bed!' You even got them in your clothes.' She held out the husk of an empty shell.

'Tch, tch, tch!' a tongue clicked reprovingly near Amrita's ear.

Amrita swung round. 'Hanuman?' she whispered. 'Are you here?'

'Am I here? Am I there? Am I anywhere?'

She felt the breath of his voice tickling her cheek and the back of her neck.

'You cheeky monkey!' she chortled. 'It was you playing tricks on me.' She heard a rustle of leaves above her head and the sound of scampering. She caught a glimpse of tail and a twitch of ears in a cherry tree along the road. 'Are we going to rescue Sita?'

'Buy your dress first!' ordered Hanuman's voice in her ear. 'You have to look right for the occasion.'

'Oh, but I'll never look right in what Granny will buy me. How I hate dresses.'

'Wear a salvar kameez. That is much more suitable,' suggested Hanuman.

'She'll never let me. Granny just loves frilly dresses.'

'Hmm! We'll see about that!' muttered

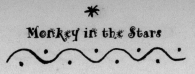

Hanuman.

They reached the High Street. After gazing into the windows of several saree and dress shops, Granny steered Amrita into Rita's Sweeter Maid which specialised in clothes for girls.

At Granny's request, Rita brought out all her frilliest dresses, and Amrita had to try on one after the other. Each time, she came out of the cubicle and stood in front of the mirror to be judged by her grandmother. In the reflection, she glimpsed a swish of tail disappearing among the racks of clothes and long black fingers whisking through the hangers. She caught beady black eyes peering at her between the hanging garments.

'This one?' Amrita asked Hanuman silently.

'Terrible!' His face screwed up with disgust time after time, because, as soon as Amrita stood in front of the long mirror, the dress she wore looked like rags.

Even when Amrita put on the bright pink dress, stiff as newly spun candy floss on a stick, with layers of net petticoat, and bright sequins which sparkled on the bodice, and large floppy bows which bounced on each sleeve, Granny

looked puzzled. 'I don't understand it. You look like a rag-doll. It looked so nice on the hanger . . . Rita is losing her touch, I tell you. What to do?'

Then Hanuman, who had been hiding behind a whole rack of clothes, help up a beautiful salvar kameez and shook it at Amrita. 'This one, this one!' he whispered. It was cotton and silk and softly yellow like a ripening mango; it had delicate embroidery round the neck and sleeves like the twining tracery of laced marble; the dupatta was light and flowing, pouring over her arms like water as she took it from him.

'May I try this, Granny?' she asked.

'Well . . .' Granny liked the bright pink, frilly dress, but surprised even herself by changing her mind. 'You can try it, dear – but . . . go, go, go, be quick about it. We can't hang about all day.'

When Amrita appeared from the changing-room, Granny couldn't say a word, and Rita was flabbergasted. 'Goodness me! I didn't even know I had such a salvar kameez. How could I forget? It fits as though it were made for you. She's got to have this outfit, I tell you.'

Granny nodded and finally spoke in a hushed

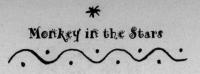

voice, 'Yes, you're right. It makes her look quite pretty. Yes, yes, child. That's the one for Diwali.'

The new salvar kameez hung from the hanger on the back of Amrita's bedroom door. She could see it from her bed. Moonbeams fell upon it, threading themselves in and out of the pale yellow material so that it glistened.

'It's time to put it on.' Hanuman's voice filled the room like an aroma of honeysuckle and evening air. Amrita obeyed. When she was dressed and had combed out her hair, she stood in the window and stared down at the dark garden. Hanuman came bounding out of the starry sky, his tail trailing like a comet and, this time, Amrita leapt fearlessly on to his back.

Chapter Four

The Final Conflict

RAVANA GROUND HIS TEETH. IN EVERY corner of India, in all the cities, towns and villages, in the lonely expanses of the desert, along the shores of the ocean, up in the chilly peaks of the Himalayas, people were building models of him. They were tall, evil-looking likenesses with ten heads, red glaring eyes, tongues dripping with blood and twenty arms which flayed in all directions.

When they finished building the models, they stuck them up on a high platform and carried them through the streets to the banks of a river, where they burnt them and cast the ashes into the water.

'Huh!' sneered Ravana. 'Think they can get rid of me, do they? Don't they realise nobody can kill me?'

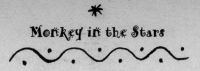
Ravana took up his veena and began to play, his many fingers strumming the strings. No one played like him. His sounds enchanted all who listened.

Ravana was sad. He knew that many would obey him, many would flatter him, many would fear him. But no one would love him. He longed for Sita's love. Her beauty and goodness flowed like honey. But she was Rama's wife and she loved her husband.

Rama. The name filled Ravana with fury. He strode to the ramparts of his palace and looked out across the ocean to the dark shores of the mainland. He knew that Rama was gathering an army to come and fight him and rescue Sita. An army of monkeys and bears with long sharp nails and ripping teeth. He looked at the heaving ocean and smiled; that was his greatest protection. Monkeys can't swim; bears can't fly. How would they cross the sea? He was safe.

Ravana stretched out his twenty arms. He stretched and stretched until he became as broad as the night, and all his twenty eyes became just one all-seeing eye. Then, in a vast quilt of darkness and

plucking strings, he rolled himself over the surface of the earth.

Amrita had heard the wonderful music, and she and Hanuman danced among the stars.

'Where does the music come from?' she asked breathlessly.

'It is Ravana,' answered Hanuman. 'He was given the gift of music before he became bad, when he was loved by the Creator, Lord Vishnu. Now, it is the only good thing he has left, and he plays to remember what he once was.'

When they crossed the Himalayas, Hanuman carried Amrita southwards over the darkening land. At the far edge of the ocean, where the sea sparkled in the setting sun, Amrita saw that the shore was swarming with monkeys. They seemed to be building a bridge.

Hanuman crossed the ocean and landed on the island of Lanka. He made himself and Amrita invisible so they could search for Sita.

A hush hung over the demon city but, lined on the ramparts of the palace, the demon warriors sharpened their weapons and waited.

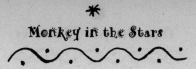

Hanuman and Amrita couldn't find Sita. She was no longer in the garden. They went into every chamber in the palace, from the highest terraces, down to the cellars in the bowels of the earth. At last, they found her in the deepest, darkest dungeon. The light from Hanuman's eyes cast a soft glow. Sita crouched in a corner, her face on her knees.

'Ah, Princess!' he sighed and bowed respectfully. 'We have found you. Be brave. It won't be long now before you are rescued.'

Sita's pale face gleamed sadly in the darkness.

'I want you to stay here with Sita,' said Hanuman to Amrita.

For the first time, Amrita was afraid. 'Don't leave me,' she pleaded. 'It's so dark.'

'Sita needs you,' said the Monkey God. 'All over the world battles are about to begin. Light will win over Darkness; Good over Evil; Prince Rama over Ravana. Stay with Sita and give her courage for the sound of battle will be terrifying.'

'Yes, yes, of course I will stay,' whispered Amrita. She knelt down by the Princess Sita. 'I'll stay with you until Rama comes.'

91

Sita smiled, then Hanuman was gone and they were plunged into pitch darkness.

The battle was terrible. All through the day and night and the next day, the ground shuddered beneath their feet. Sita and Amrita huddled in the darkness. They thought the universe was being destroyed.

Who was winning and who was losing? Could Rama kill Ravana? Every time he struck off one head, another grew in its place. But Rama finally took up his special golden arrow. He fitted it to his bow and aimed at Ravana's heart.

An almighty crash shook every stone in the city. Sita and Amrita thought the end of the world had come. The stillness was like the quiet after a storm, when the rain has stopped and the thunder has died away. What had happened? Would someone come to rescue them? Neither dared speak.

Then, without warning, the great door burst open. A blinding shaft of daylight cut across the floor. A figure, tall as a giant filled the doorway.

Amrita's head stayed bowed, not daring to see who stood before them, but Sita raised her eyes,

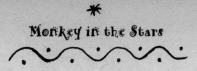
and as they adjusted to the brightness, she gave a cry of joy. 'Hanuman!'

Hanuman held out his hand to Sita. 'Ravana is dead! Come, Princess! Your husband, Prince Rama, is waiting for you.'

Rama and Sita were reunited and their fourteen years in the jungle were over. They could go home to the Kingdom of Ayodhya.

Chapter Five

Diwali

HANUMAN CARRIED AMRITA OVER THE world. Below them, they saw people dressed in their new Diwali clothes, greeting each other on the streets; they saw the exchange of presents and sweets; they saw the young men lighting fireworks and the girls shrieking with delight. And as night began to fall, they saw the thousands upon thousands of little saucers of wicks and oil being placed along verandas and steps, window ledges and balconies, to light the way for Rama and Sita on their long journey back home.

'It's time for you to go back too, Amrita,' said Hanuman softly. 'It is Diwali the Festival of Light and the New Year. You must be ready for the Goddess Lakshmi to come into your home.'

Below them, the grey towns and cities still

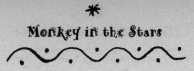
slept. Thousands of homes had been scrubbed clean. Hedges had been cut and paths swept. And in front of thousands of homes there were rangoli patterns made from sprinkled rice flour and coloured spice powders. As they came closer to Amrita's house, they saw that her mother and aunt had created a beautiful pattern outside the front door and, edging the paths and lawns and all the windowsills, were rows of saucers of oil waiting to be lit.

'Yes!' murmured Hanuman approvingly. 'Your household is ready for Diwali. Lakshmi can come here.'

Amrita slid back into her bedroom, then turned to Hanuman hovering in space outside her window. He was shining, silver — the Monkey God. She wanted to speak, but had no words, so she clasped her hands in reverence and thanks.

Hanuman smiled and raised a hand in farewell, then he too, pressed his palms together in a namaste — and was gone.

The next day Amrita helped her mother and grandmother as they prepared for the big Diwali

party they were holding at their house that evening. Wonderful smells of cooking wafted through the house; platters of bhaji and pakoras, kofti and spiced sausages were carried through. Naan bread and poories, rice and lentils, spiced vegetables and salad creations soon crowded the party table.

Darkness fell. The excitement grew. Grandmother and mother went out with long, burning tapers, and lit the little oil-lamps. Amrita put on her special Diwali salvar kameez. The guests began to arrive – gleaming as though they were new-born; fresh as if they had sprung into creation in their glittering new clothes.

As the party got going, chatter and laughter mixing in with music and singing, Amrita crept silently upstairs. Suddenly, she wanted to be alone, and to remember everything that had happened with Hanuman.

The party ended, the guests went home and the house became still, as sleep overcame everyone. Outside, the oil-lamps still glimmered. Amrita stared out into the black night. The darkness extended into eternity. Her eye fixed upon a

strange creamy light. It grew brighter and brighter and brighter. It increased with an energy which seemed to come from all the gods put together: from Agni, the God of Fire, Varun, the God of Water; it came from Brahma, Shiva and Vishnu; from the mountains and the oceans and from all creation. The light was swirling like churned milk. Out of the churning rose Lakshmi, floating on a golden lotus flower. She looked like Sita; she was Sita. Sita was Lakshmi, the great Goddess of Wealth and Prosperity. Energy flowed from her feet, arms, waist, thighs, nose, teeth, eyes and throat. She paused for a moment over the rangoli pattern at the threshold as if to admire it — then swept inside. Her light filled the house and, for a moment, it seemed as though Amrita's house was the very centre of the universe. Then Lakshmi was gone, gently rippling away into the night, and all that was left was the scent of flowers.

When Amrita woke the next morning, there was a scattering of monkey-nut shells and blossom across her carpet. She knew that every year the battle between Good and Evil would be fought out again and again, so long as the world existed. But

for one of those battles, Amrita had been there.

As she stood before the mirror and brushed out her hair, she heard a faint clapping. A monkey-nut flew through the air and struck her on the shoulder. Amrita laughed out loud, 'I know you're there, Hanuman!' She ran to the window. The bough of the apple tree was swaying. She glimpsed a long silver tail. It swished and twitched and then was still.

The Girl
Who Rode
on a Lion

The Story of Durga

Chapter One
The Arrival

ONCE, IT LOOKED LIKE A HILL. IT MUST have been a thickly wooded hill, with deep undergrowth. It must have been inhabited by rabbits and hares and squirrels and foxes; and rooks nesting in the tree-tops and owls hooting at midnight.

Now, you wouldn't know it had been a hill. It was just part of one big, sprawling city; and if owls hooted at night, no one heard them because of the traffic. The brown earth was smothered by pavements, the trees all but gone, destroyed by streets and houses and office blocks, and, of course, people. So many people.

This was the city to which Durga came. Yet somehow she knew the ground on which she walked and what it had been. It was as though the

spirit of the earth called to her through her feet. Somewhere, she could hear the pulse, beating like a drum. She could hear the rushing of streams and the wind whipping up the branches of the trees before the rain.

That night, Anil swore he saw a fox. Something woke him. He got out of bed without putting on the light, and went to the window.

There was a full moon; a brighter than bright moon on which it was possible to see all the mountains and craters on its surface. Its shine made the slates of the roofs glitter like waves and turned the trunks of the garden trees to silver.

Then he saw the fox. There it stood, bold as anything, staring up at the house. It seemed as though the moonlight caught the tips of every single hair on its body so that it glowed.

All the curtains of the house were drawn to, except one. The smallest window of the smallest spare bedroom at the back of the house; its curtains were not drawn, because the person who was going to sleep in that room hadn't yet arrived.

But it was as if everything was waiting for her; the garden, the trees, the moon and the fox. All

were waiting for a girl called Durga.

Although she was expected, when the doorbell rang the next morning and there was a strange girl standing on the doorstep with a suitcase at her side, everyone was taken by surprise.

It was Kiki who answered the door. She hesitated on the threshold, looking puzzled. Who was this girl, so small, so wizened, with a slight hunch on her back and looking like a gnome? Her arms were thin, her wrists bony, and her fingers like the stripped twigs of winter trees.

But when the girl looked her straight in the face and said, 'Hello, I'm Durga,' there was nothing faltering about her gaze. Her large black eyes seemed to suck everything into their depths. She studied Kiki. Although they were the same age, ten years old, Kiki was taller and chubbier, and her hair was cropped as short as a boy's. She was dressed in jeans, a T-shirt and the latest pair of pink trainers, yet for all her tomboy looks, she hung back timidly and appeared afraid of getting things wrong.

For some moments, Kiki stared back, mesmerized. Then suddenly she unfroze, and

abandoning the girl still on the doorstep, fled back to the kitchen where the rest of the family were having breakfast.

'Mum! Mum! It's Durga! She's come!' Mother frowned, and she and Father looked at each other.

'I thought you said she was coming tomorrow,' said Father.

'I thought so too. It's what my sister said, but then she's always been such a scatterbrain.'

Anil leapt up from the table, his mouth stuffed with toast, and pushing roughly past Kiki, ran to gape at the girl waiting patiently at the front door.

'Are you Durga?' he demanded. 'You're not supposed to be here till tomorrow.'

Anil stared at her rudely. This was not the sort of person he wanted to acknowledge as a cousin. Not only did he think her extremely ugly, but she was wearing a tunic, pyjamas and veil. No one dressed like that round here. Even his mother only wore a saree for special occasions.

'No, I was meant to come now,' said Durga firmly. 'My parents have gone on to the airport and will soon be on an aeroplane flying to India.'

Heaving up her suitcase, she stepped inside the

hall and removed her shoes. At that moment, Mother appeared. She was looking flustered, and trying not to frown. 'Durga, my dear!' she exclaimed, embracing the girl with as much warmth as she could muster. 'We weren't expecting you till tomorrow. Who dropped you? Why didn't they stay and say hello? Have your parents gone to the airport today? How silly. We must have misunderstood. I was sure you were coming tomorrow. Anyway, come in, my dear!'

'I'm sorry, Aunty Meena,' murmured Durga apologetically.

'She's taken her shoes off!' scoffed Anil. 'Why did you do that?'

'We always do at home. Don't you?' said Durga. 'Otherwise you bring the dirt in from outside.'

Anil opened his mouth and shut it again. Then Father appeared, followed by Kiki, who hung back shyly behind him.

'Ah, Durga!' he boomed, brushing the toast crumbs from his tie. 'You seem to have caught us unexpectedly. We thought you were coming tomorrow. I'm afraid your aunt and I are rushing

off to work so we can't stay and see you in properly. Luckily, Anil and Kiki have a day off from school today – teacher training or something – and we have our au pair, Ulrike. She'll look after you. She's German and a very nice girl.' He indicated a smiling young woman who stood at the sink washing up.

As he spoke, Mr and Mrs Dalal pulled on their coats and picked up their briefcases. He was a surgeon and worked at the regional hospital. She was a solicitor, and had an office to go to. He went out, calling 'Goodbye,' climbed into his big silver car and drove away. Then Mother, after giving each child a peck on the cheek and a reminder to be good, drove off in a smaller red car and said she would see them later. She instructed her children and Ulrike to look after Durga and help her to settle into her room.

So that was the manner in which Durga arrived to stay with her cousins for the next three months, while her parents and baby brother visited relatives in India.

Kiki stole an admiring look at her cousin. She thought to herself, I would surely be crying my

head off if I was left with cousins for three months. Especially cousins I didn't know and might not even like. But Durga seemed so calm, even when Anil did his usual beastly boastful thing.

'There is one rule in this house which you must obey,' he told her. 'No one is allowed in my room without my permission. See?' As Ulrike led Durga upstairs to her room followed by Kiki and Anil, Anil pointed to the large notice pinned on his door. It said: DO NOT ENTER ON PAIN OF DEATH.

'Anyone who disobeys gets beaten up,' he snarled threateningly.

'I wouldn't dream of going in,' said Durga.

'I've got a notice on my door too, but Anil takes no notice. He's always barging in,' complained Kiki.

Ulrike was nice. She had a kind, round rosy face with long blonde hair tied into one shining neat plait. She took Durga into the small guest room and lifted her suitcase on to the table to unpack.

There was one small bed, a wardrobe, a chest of drawers and an upright chair. Otherwise the room

was bare.

'We'll soon fill it with all your things,' said Ulrike comfortingly. 'Then it will be like home.'

'It will never be like my room, of course,' declared Anil. 'I've got my own television, computer, printer and music centre. Sometimes I let Kiki in to play computer games with me, but I always beat her. Do you play?'

Durga shrugged. 'Maybe,' she murmured.

'You can play on my computer if you like,' said Kiki warmly.

'Huh!' snorted Anil. 'She's got my old computer. It's not half as powerful as mine, and she only plays silly baby games.'

'Is that all you've got?' exclaimed Ulrike when Durga opened up her suitcase. Even Kiki was amazed. Durga only had three or four sets of tunics and pyjamas, three cardigans and some underwear. Kiki's cupboards were stuffed with clothes – so much that she hardly ever knew what to wear.

'Are you poor?' asked Anil.

'Anil! Don't be so rude!' cried Kiki.

'What's so rude about that?' I only asked. She's

got hardly anything. Haven't you got any trainers or jeans or things like that?'

'Anil, why don't you go and play on your computer while Durga unpacks,' suggested Ulrike, firmly pushing him towards the door.

'I don't have to,' retorted Anil, roughly shaking her off.

'You do if Durga says so. It's her room now,' reminded Kiki.

'No it's not. She's just using it. She's only a visitor,' Anil argued.

'Anil! Out!' repeated Ulrike, grabbing his arm.

'You can't make me!' he shouted, trying to shake her off.

'But I can, Anil,' said Durga quietly, and she turned and fixed her eyes upon him.

'Anil, please go.'

Anil seemed to lose all power of speech and movement, as he felt himself swallowed up into the depths of her deep black eyes . . . Two eyes . . . or . . . was it three? Something . . . almost the shape of an eye . . . seemed to shimmer in the middle of her forehead; but the minute he thought he saw it, the eye disappeared. It could have been

the passing of a split second, or an eternity, Anil wouldn't have known. Only when Durga turned away swiftly was he released from her gaze. Obediently he left the room.

It didn't take long to put away Durga's clothes. Then Ulrike said, 'Have you anything to stick on the walls? They look so bare. Kiki and Anil have lots of pictures and posters.'

'I just have this,' said Durga taking out a thin poster which had lain tightly rolled in her suitcase.

'Let's see!' begged Kiki, full of curiosity. Durga slowly and carefully unrolled her picture. Ulrike and Kiki stared in amazement.

'Who's that?' breathed Kiki in wonderment.

She was looking at a brightly coloured picture of a beautiful woman gazing serenely out at the world, even though she had ten arms which whirled around her, and even though she sat on a ferocious-looking lion which snarled with outstretched claws.

'I don't think I'd want that in my bedroom, it would give me nightmares,' laughed Ulrike.

'Oh no, I feel safer,' Durga assured her. 'It's the

goddess Durga. I was named after her because she fights for peace and friendship.'

That night Anil had a dream. At least, he thought it was a dream.

Once more, he was looking out of his window. Once more, he saw the fox standing in the moonlight; but then a huge shadow emerged out of the undergrowth.

It was an animal that seemed almost as big as the garden. Its great body crossed the moonlit lawn in just two paces, and then with red, burning eyes, it stared up at the small, spare bedroom window, just as the fox had done the previous night. But this time, the animal was not a fox, but a huge, powerful, golden lion.

Anil would have told everyone about it the next morning, only he forgot.

Chapter Two

Fear at the School Gates

EVEN KIKI, WHO WAS A KIND GIRL, FELT a little embarrassed going to school with Durga the next day. Anil wouldn't walk with them at all. 'I don't want people knowing she's part of our family. They'll laugh,' he declared.

Mother had tried to find some suitable school clothes for Durga. 'No one wears tunic and pyjamas in Kiki's school,' she explained. But all Kiki's clothes were too big, so Durga went in her own clothes anyway.

'I'll ask Ulrike to take you shopping after school to buy you some clothes so that you won't feel the odd one out at school.'

'Oh, I don't mind,' said Durga. 'I'd feel more strange having to wear a skirt and blouse.' But her aunt wouldn't hear of it. Durga might not mind,

111

but she did; after all, she had to think of her neighbours. This was a good area where they had never experienced any prejudice, and Mrs Dalal was sure this was because they had fitted in. She and Mr Dalal dressed in Western clothes bought from shops like Austin Reed and Jaeger. She only wore sarees in the evening because they made her look like an exotic princess. This delighted people, so long as it was only in the evening.

He belonged to the golf club and she to the Women's Institute; they were regular hosts and guests to others in the neighbourhood, and Mrs Dalal made sure that her house didn't smell of curry too often.

Their motto, as Mr Dalal often intoned, was, 'When in Rome do as the Romans do. Then you'll be accepted.'

Unfortunately, this was not what their children had experienced, though they never dared tell their father.

Although Kiki had never worn anything else except jeans and T-shirts and skirts and blouses, she only had a few friends at school and no one ever asked her home. Mumtaz was her best friend,

but because Mumtaz lived on the other side of town and anyway had to attend Moslem school every evening, they never played after school. Only little Clare from next door, though she went to a different school, sometimes popped in to play.

As for Anil, the situation was even worse. Not even Kiki knew how bad. He was such a bully and a boaster at home that she was sure that was how he must be at school, and she wasn't in the least surprised that he had no friends.

He went to Phoenix House School, the best that money could buy. Mr Dalal urged him to work hard, holding out the prospect of success and prosperity if he did. At home, Anil gave every impression of being the success his parents desired.

'I came top again in maths,' he would tell them, 'and Mr Benson says I could win the history prize this year.'

How his parents loved hearing news like that. His father's eyes would glow with pride, and his mother would softly stroke his hair and give him hugs.

'See, Kiki? See how well your brother does? I hope it will be an inspiration for you to improve.

To think you were almost bottom of the class last year!' her parents would say.

Then Kiki would bow her head meekly and promise to try harder.

Now, on their way to school, Ulrike and Durga walked together. Kiki dawdled a little way behind, but Anil strode on, metres ahead, as if he wasn't with them at all. But the closer they got to school, the harder and bigger the lump of fear grew in Anil's stomach. He knew who would be waiting for him.

Kiki's school came first. That meant Anil always had to walk the last half-mile on his own. When they came to Kiki's school gates, the girls turned to say goodbye to him. Ulrike was going in with them to introduce Durga to the teachers. Kiki just yelled, 'Bye, Anil!' and skipped on ahead into school. Ulrike waved cheerily at him and followed Kiki. Only Durga looked him in the eye.

'They won't have seen anyone as peculiar as you before,' he hissed nastily, and turned to go on his way. But he had only gone a few paces when he stopped and looked back. Durga was still standing there watching him. It was as if her gaze

could see right into his head and read his
thoughts; and it was as if she knew that he had
a great lump of fear inside him, as he braced
himself to meet his enemies. He walked on, but
before he turned the corner, he looked back once
more. She was still standing there gazing at him.
Even from that distance, he had the strangest
impression that a third eye slowly materialized and
gazed at him, glowing in the middle of her
forehead. But the minute he thought it, the eye
vanished. He forgot what he had seen and
continued on his way.

'Well!' the big boy demanded. 'What have you
got for us?'

There were three of them; Goutam, Carl and
Ricky. They waited in a menacing group, shoulder
to shoulder, blocking Anil's way.

Every day they were there. Every day they
demanded something before they would let him
pass. At first it was money. Whatever he had in his
pocket. But then, because he only had fifty pence
or so, they said they wanted more. Cigarettes, for
instance. He told them that no one in his family
smoked, but that didn't make any difference.

'You'll just have to buy us some, smelly-face,' they had snarled.

'But I don't have enough money for that!' Anil protested.

'That's your lookout. We don't care if you steal them, just have some cigarettes for us tomorrow.'

So the nightmare began and continued day after day after day. Anil thought it would never end. When his pocket money was no longer enough, he took to stealing from his mother's purse. But then she got puzzled, when she found she had less than she thought, and became suspicious; perhaps she even wondered if Ulrike was pinching from her, and she stopped leaving her bag around.

At last the day came when Anil stole from the newsagent just near his school. It was run by old Mr Patel. Anil would ask him for a small bag of humbugs. He knew this meant that Mr Patel must turn his back for a few moments, to reach up for the tall glass jar of stripy sweets, which stood on an upper shelf. It was then that Anil would nip round the counter and snatch a packet of cigarettes. He couldn't always get away with this;

especially if there were other people in the shop, so then Anil would have to think of something else.

Goutam said, 'Your mother's bound to have some jewellery. That'll do as well as cigarettes, won't it, Carl?' He conferred with his fellow extortionists.

'Yeah!' agreed Carl and Ricky. 'So long as it's not junk from Woolies or the market. Proper jewellery; that's what we want. Gold.'

'Oh, she'll have gold all right,' confirmed Goutam. 'Women like her always do.'

At first, Anil tried to refuse. He tried to stand up to them and push past them into school. That's when they jumped on him like a pack of wolves.

'You little weasel! You just try something like that again and we'll rip your guts out.' They squeezed their fingers round his throat and twisted his arms till he thought they would break.

He had gone into school trying not to show that he had been crying. He could hardly concentrate in class and came bottom in the weekly French test. Nowadays, when he got home each evening, the only way he could make himself feel better, brave enough to face the bullies the

next day, was to bully Kiki.

'Well?' demanded the boys at the gate. 'What has our little weasel got for us today?'

They had been sitting on a high wall, smoking. Now they dropped to the ground and surrounded him, pushing their mean faces up against his.

Anil put his hand in his pocket. Today he had stolen a pair of his father's gold cuff-links. His father hardly ever wore them. He had declared that he found them too fussy, but as they were a gift from his wife's parents, he wore them when they visited. Anil hoped they wouldn't visit for a long time, and that his father wouldn't mind anyway if he couldn't find them.

'Huh! Not bad,' murmured Goutam, holding them in the outspread palm of his hand. Ricky and Carl always let Goutam examine the jewellery. He seemed to know the value of things, and got a good price for them when he sold them in the town.

'Yeah! These are gold. I reckon I'll get a few quid for these.'

That evening, Anil came home from school like a tornado. He slammed into the house, chucked

his bag across the kitchen floor, refused to eat his tea, and barged upstairs into Kiki's room. Kiki pounded after him screaming her protests.

'Get out! Get out of my room, you big fat bully!' she cried.

'You can't stop me! I'll go where I please. Anyway, I feel like playing on my computer,' bellowed Anil.

'That computer's mine. You gave it to me!' cried Kiki.

'I didn't give it. I only lent it. It's still mine. If you want to call it yours, then you'd better pay for it. I want a hundred pounds; otherwise it's still mine.'

'I hate you, I hate you!' shrieked Kiki, tears beginning to pour down her cheeks. She hurled herself on top of her brother, punching and kicking.

Durga and Ulrike rushed to try and stop the quarrel. At that moment, Anil broke free of his sister's clutching fingers and, grabbing a book, hurled it at her with all his might. The book missed. It flew through the open doorway and struck an ornamental china plate which was

hanging on the landing wall. The plate crashed to the floor and broke into a hundred little pieces.

There was a horrible silence. Then Anil shouted, 'Look what you've done, you stupid girl!'

Ulrike finally managed to restore some order. She told the children to go to their own rooms. They all waited with dread for the parents to come home.

Kiki's bedroom overlooked the street. Miserably, she looked out of the window and watched the straggle of children getting off the bus which had brought them from the school down the hill. A lot of the girls were wearing tunics and pyjamas. They were all chatting easily in groups and looked so happy. Suddenly Kiki longed to join them. She wasn't part of a group like that at her school, and hardly anyone went home on the bus.

Children at her school were mostly met at the school gates by mothers or fathers or au pairs in shiny smart cars, and were whisked away to their large expensive houses. Often the girls invited each other to tea, but no one ever invited Kiki; and when she invited them, they nearly always had an

excuse not to come.

She saw her mother's red car turn into their drive. Kiki didn't rush down to greet her with a hug. Instead she waited and listened. She heard the front door close, and as it did, Anil flew down the stairs shouting cheerily, 'Hi Mum! Guess what! I got an A for geography.' He didn't give any credit to Ulrike, who had spent hours helping him with his homework.

'Oh Anil! You clever boy,' cooed his mother, clasping him in her arms. 'Your father will be pleased.'

Kiki crept out onto the landing and peered down through the bannisters. Her mother and Anil went into the kitchen where Ulrike and Durga were getting tea ready.

'Ulrike! Did you go and buy Durga some clothes for school, as I asked?'

'No, Mrs Dalal. I'm sorry, I didn't. Something came up and it wasn't possible.'

'But Ulrike, that's too bad! I wanted this done. It's very important. What happened?' cried Mrs Dalal in an annoyed voice.

'Kiki broke your best plate,' smirked Anil.

'Oh Anil, that's not quite true,' cried Ulrike.

But her words were drowned by Mrs Dalal's cry of dismay. 'Which plate? Not the special Viennese plate up on the landing? Oh no! The stupid child! She'll pay for this. Kiki! Kiki! Come down here immediately!'

Kiki sat frozen at the top of the stairs. Her mother ran up angrily. She stared at the gap on the wall, and noted the pieces of plate wrapped in a newspaper and placed on a table for her to see. She turned on her daughter and smacked her hard.

'You naughty girl! Do you realise that you've destroyed a work of art? That plate was invaluable! I'll never have another.'

She raised her hand ready to strike again, but suddenly Durga's voice interrupted.

'It wasn't Kiki's fault, really it wasn't. It was an accident.'

Mrs Dalal's hand fell to her side. She looked down the stairs to where Durga stood at the bottom. Mrs Dalal found herself staring straight into Durga's large eyes, and for a moment, she almost fancied that she saw a third eye appear in the middle of her forehead; but the minute she

thought it, it disappeared.

She walked more slowly and calmly down the stairs.

'Ulrike,' she said. 'There's still an hour before the shops close. Take my car and drive into town with Durga. Buy her a navy blue skirt, a white blouse and a navy cardigan. You can get it all at Foster's, and tell them to put it on my account.'

That night, Mr and Mrs Dalal had a talk.

'I can't find those gold cuff-links your mother gave me,' he said with a frown. 'It's not that I like them very much, but I wanted to wear them to a business dinner I have tomorrow night. I thought they would be suitable.'

'Yes, I've noticed some things have gone missing,' murmured Mrs Dalal. 'I can't find a gold bracelet. It's simply not in my jewellery case. I've looked absolutely everywhere. Then there's a brooch and a pair of earrings. All of them cost a pretty penny.'

'What do you think?' asked Mr Dalal, 'Could it be Ulrike?'

Mrs Dalal shook her head unhappily. 'I just

don't know. I keep hoping I'll find a reasonable explanation, but now I'm beginning to wonder.'

She got out of bed restlessly, and wandered over to the window. It was a wild and windy night outside. Dark clouds were racing across the sky, and the moon seemed to be tossed this way and that. She thought she saw a slight figure standing in the middle of the lawn.

'Durga? I that Durga?' she exclaimed.

'Eh?' grunted her husband sleepily. 'What are you on about?'

'I could have sworn I saw Durga standing on the lawn.'

Yet the minute she said it, the wind gusted up and tossed the branches of the sycamore tree in whirling shadows across the grass. She shivered and went back to bed. So she never saw the golden lion step out across the garden, nor did she see Durga climb up on to his back.

Chapter Three

A Face in the Mirror

KIKI WAS AMAZED THAT IT ONLY SEEMED to take Durga a few days to settle in at school. Even though she was so strange and different, and had come to school at first wearing tunic and pyjamas; even though she looked so odd with her thin little body and hunched back, all the children seemed to like her. She moved incredibly fast and loved joining in the tag games in the playground. She had a face which made people want to be friends with her because she smiled a lot and laughed easily; and she was clever, very, very clever. She could do the more difficult sums straight out of her head and her writing was beautiful. Yet Durga wasn't boastful and was always ready to help. Every night, she helped Kiki a lot with her homework, and that left them

125

plenty of time to play, especially on the computer.

'I wasn't ever any good at the computer,' Kiki told her. 'Anil is so much quicker and better than me.'

Anil came bursting in one afternoon while they were playing a game. He was surprised to see how fast Kiki had become.

'Get off, let me have a go,' he cried roughly, pushing her aside. 'I bet I can beat that score easily.'

He did beat Kiki, though only just, and then Kiki said, 'I bet you can't beat Durga.'

'Bet I can!' shouted Anil boastfully. 'Come on, Durga! See if you can beat my score!'

Durga shrugged and sat before the screen. The game that came up was called 'Catch the Monkey'.

'Go!' commanded Anil.

Durga's fingers began to tap.

Anil leaned forward in astonishment. He knew he had fast fingers, but he had never seen anything like this before. Durga's fingers tapped away so fast that you could hardly see them, and her eye anticipated every move the little figures made on the screen. Within 60 seconds she had a score of 1500. It was unbelievable.

'You must be cheating somehow!' yelled Anil jealously.

'Have another go,' suggested Durga, giving up her place.

With a sulky pout, Anil sat before the screen and tried again. To his surprise, his fingers moved like the wind, and though he didn't beat Durga's score, he beat his own record.

'Hmm,' he murmured, feeling lots better. 'I nearly beat you. I probably will tomorrow.'

'Durga,' said Kiki shyly, taking her cousin's hand. 'I like having you here. I wish you'd live with us forever.'

Was it true that since Durga's arrival Anil seemed to have become, by a few degrees, just a little nicer? Did he not quarrel with Kiki quite so much, and not boast quite so much? And yet, Anil couldn't feel really better inside – not while he was a thief, not while he was a victim of those bullies. Every day he had to confront Goutam and his gang at the school gates with something he had stolen for them. Every night he dreaded his nightmares.

When animals are in pain, when they are aching with hunger or grief-stricken at the loss of

their young, they creep into their burrows deep in the ground, so that the kind earth always knows about their sadness. It can feel their suffering, hear their cries and soak up their tears.

But who is there to hear the sobs of lonely children in the night? Who would hear Anil, with his face buried in his pillow, soaking it with tears?

His parents couldn't hear, for their bedroom was divided from his by the bathroom; Kiki didn't hear, because she slept on the other side of the house; Ulrike didn't hear, because her room was up in the roof, in the loft conversion; and why should Durga hear, when her bedroom was furthest away along the corridor?

But Durga did hear. Just as the earth receives messages from the roots of trees or the wailing wind; just as it sees and hears and feels the throb of all living things, so Durga felt Anil's pain.

Though she lay in her bed asleep, a sharp clear beam of light pierced the darkness of the night. It came from the third eye which had opened in the middle of Durga's forehead.

Anil moaned in his sleep and rolled over. His dreams had been troubled. He had been pursued

by Goutam, Carl and Ricky. They were twisting his arms and hurting him. Then there was his teacher's face looming over his work.

'Oh dear, oh dear, oh dear!' His teacher's voice grated sarcastically. 'What kind of nonsense have we here? You haven't understood this at all. I can only give you four out of ten. What will your parents say when I see them on parents' evening?'

Anil groaned. What would they say? What would they say?

Then he saw Durga's face. He didn't know if it was in a dream or in his mind's eye. 'How strange,' he thought. 'Why did I think she was ugly?' As she looked at him with such kindness and friendship, a third eye came shimmering into the middle of her forehead, and the sharp light which came from it seemed to wipe out all his fears. He gave a deep sigh, and fell fast asleep again.

The next morning, Anil didn't remember his night terrors, nor his dream about Durga. He awoke in a daze, and automatically wondered what he could steal for his tormentors today.

He got up and went to the bathroom. He paused outside his parents' bedroom.

They were usually both downstairs by this time. This was when he had had the opportunity to slip inside and rifle through the dressing table drawers.

But this morning, they were both still in their room, talking in low voices. He heard the word 'steal'. It made him stop and listen. Then he felt himself go hot and cold with fear and remorse both at once.

'It must be Ulrike,' his mother was saying. 'I'll have to confront her.'

'It's terrible,' murmured Father. 'I can hardly believe it of her. She's been the best au pair we've ever had. It just shows, you can't trust anyone these days.'

'I won't do anything now. Let's deal with it tonight when the children have gone to bed.'

'I agree,' said Father. 'We don't want them to witness an unpleasant scene.'

Anil felt turned to stone. 'Ulrike. They think Ulrike is a thief. She'll be sent away.'

'Are you all right, Anil?' asked Ulrike, as he came into the kitchen. 'You took a long time getting ready. You look pale. I hope you're not sickening

130

for something.' She went over to him and checked his forehead with her hand.

He pushed her off impatiently, and then felt ashamed. The best thing about Ulrike was that she never bore a grudge. Even when he had been rude to her, she never let a bad atmosphere linger for too long.

He hung his head. He felt a confession rushing to his lips. He wanted to cry out, 'Ulrike, I did it. I stole all those things. But my parents think it's you. They'll send you away . . .'

But he couldn't. He hadn't quite got the courage. He just replied in a gruff voice, 'Of course I'm all right.'

He snatched the cornflakes for himself just as Kiki was reaching for them.

'I think it would serve him right if he got mumps or something really nasty,' sniped Kiki.

Anil caught Durga's eye. He was going to say something mean, but the words died on his lips, and instead he flopped at the table and shook the cornflakes into a bowl. He felt numb inside. Helpless.

Mother and Father came down. Their faces

131

were solemn and restrained. They seemed to be trying to act as normal, but though they saw the children off to school as cheerily as they could, they could hardly look Ulrike in the eye, and she was overcome by a feeling of uneasiness.

Again Anil wanted to tell them everything. He wanted to cry out, 'It wasn't Ulrike who stole from you, it was me. Don't send her away!'

But he couldn't say a word, and allowed them to go off to work still believing that Ulrike was a thief.

'Come on, Anil!' Ulrike was calling him urgently. 'You're going to be late for school.'

Anil stood in his parents' bedroom. He was in front of the dressing table, guiltily looking for an item to steal for Goutam, Carl and Ricky. He opened the top drawer where his mother kept a lot of her trinkets. He fingered the necklaces and bracelets and held the earrings in the palm of his hand.

Suddenly he looked up and saw his reflection in the mirror. He was shocked, it was as though he had caught himself in the act.

He dropped the earrings back in the drawer, and as he stood staring at his own image, he was transfixed with astonishment as Durga's face

seemed to shimmer at his shoulder.

He whipped round to confront her. But there was nobody there. Only when he looked in the mirror again did he see her face staring at him. Without taking his eyes off her, Anil shut the drawer. 'I won't steal any more.' He made a sudden decision. 'I don't care what they do to me, I will not steal any more.' Instantly, Durga's face began to fade, and he forgot that he had ever seen it.

'Anil! Anil! What on earth are you doing? Come on! You'll be late for school!' Ulrike called again.

Anil leapt into action. 'I'm coming! I've just remembered something. I won't be a minute.'

He raced into his room, found a notebook and tore off a sheet of paper. Then he wrote a message to his parents and propped it in front of the mirror.

> Dear Mum and Dad,
> Please don't send Ulrike away
> She is not a thief.
> I am the one who has been stealing
> from you.
> I am very sorry, and I promise
> to pay you back one day.
> Love, Anil

133

When they reached Kiki and Durga's school, Ulrike asked Anil whether he would like her to come on to his school. She still felt a little anxious about him. She had never known him to be so quiet. When he firmly said no, she shrugged and said, 'Oh well, then I'll get the bus on into town. I have some shopping to do.'

Anil looked at Durga. Something stirred in his memory. What was it about her? Something powerful and amazing? It didn't seem possible. She stood before him, looking so odd – even odder in her new school clothes than when she wore her own. Somehow she appeared even more wizened, hunched and gnome-like than ever before. Yet the look she gave him as he left them stayed in his head. It seemed to grow and grow like a bright light, filling every crevice of his brain.

As he neared his school, he saw his enemies waiting for him. They jumped down from the wall and advanced menacingly; Goutam, Carl and Ricky. He saw their leering faces and their greedy, outstretched hands.

Anil fixed his eyes on the school gates and walked towards them. The gates are open, he said

to himself. All I have to do is walk through them. Other children were pouring through, surely he could just join them?

'Hey you! Smelly-face! Where do you think you're going? Come over here!' yelled Goutam.

Carl and Ricky strode over to Anil and blocked his path. Whichever way Anil moved, they moved with him. They were like vultures, their heads sticking forward from their necks, as if they had grown long, curved beaks and would peck him to pieces if they could. Then he felt their fingers gripping his arms, squeezing harder and harder as they forced him out of the stream of children going into school.

There was a park over the road. Anil was forced towards it. They swiftly herded him into some thick shrubbery, and when they were out of sight of the road and the school, they forced him up against a tree.

'This isn't like you, Anil!' muttered Goutam in an ugly voice. 'I never expected to have any more trouble from you. I must have made a mistake when I got the impression you were trying to avoid us. Did I get the wrong impression?'

'Answer, you horrible little weasel. Answer, or

we'll twist your arms out of their sockets!'

Carl and Ricky forced Anil's arms backwards round the tree trunk. He couldn't prevent a cry of pain breaking through his clenched teeth.

'What have you got for us today, Anil? Just hand it over and we'll let you go,' whispered Goutam, his breath hissing out as sharp as a razor.

'I haven't got anything,' gasped Anil, 'and I'm never stealing anything for you ever again.'

'Did you hear that, lads?' scoffed Goutam. 'Our little weasel says he won't steal any more. Has our little chap decided to be an angel? Are you growing wings?'

The big boys roared with laughter and began to flap their elbows and dance around him. Then they began to lunge at him, prodding and punching. Finally Carl and Ricky grabbed him and turned him upside down.

'Do you know what, Anil?' said Goutam, leering into his face. 'I have the power to make you do anything. If I want you to bark like a dog, you'll bark like a dog. If I say grunt like a pig, you'll grunt like a pig, and if I say steal, you will steal. Otherwise . . .'

Goutam left his threat hanging unfinished in the air, for at that moment, they heard a low, deep growl.

Carl and Ricky let go of Anil's legs and he fell into a heap on the ground.

'What was that?' said Carl.

'It sounded like a dog,' quavered Ricky, looking around fearfully. 'A big dog, too.'

'So what if it was a dog?' sneered Goutam. 'You're not scared of dogs, are you?'

'Depends which dog,' retorted Ricky. 'Can't say I'd go round patting pit bulls or Rottweilers.'

'I've never seen a pit bull or a Rottweiler in this park. Just little old ladies walking their poodles.'

Then the roar came again, this time from another direction.

'Hey, Goutam! That's no poodle!' gasped Carl. He and Ricky had flung themselves together, back to back.

The sound was terrifying. It started as a deep, deep gurgle, as if it came from the depths of a great throat. Then the gurgle got louder and

stronger as though the jaws of a giant mouth opened wide. It became a mighty roar and, like a clap of thunder, shook the ground with its force.

Then there was silence. Anil crouched at the base of the tree with his head in his hands. The three big boys stood in a tight cluster, back to back, looking all around and quaking with fear. Then Goutam laughed, a high-pitched giggle. 'What a bunch of wallies we must look. Come on, let's sort out Anil. We've got to teach this little sniveller a lesson.'

'Yeah,' agreed Ricky, nervously looking around, 'but let's get on with it and scram.'

It was then that Anil decided to run.

Chapter Four

A Girl on a Lion

'ANIL! KIKI! WHERE ARE YOU?' MRS Dalal had come home earlier than usual. But she had walked into an empty house and no one answered her call.

'Ulrike! Where is everyone?' she yelled again.

She went upstairs. Anil's door was open and so was Kiki's. She went along to Durga's bedroom and found herself confronted by the picture of the ten-armed goddess riding a lion. She stared at it uneasily. What was there about the goddess? The face looked familiar. Their eyes met, and wherever she walked in the room, the eyes followed her round, as she rapidly opened all the drawers and cupboards and looked under the bed. Perhaps Durga would be tempted to steal. After all, she came from a much poorer family. But Mrs Dalal

found nothing. Hurriedly, she left the room and shut the door behind her, glad to get away from the staring eyes.

Next she climbed the loft ladder into Ulrike's room. Her heart was beating fast. She felt like a burglar herself. She knew she had no right to go into Ulrike's bedroom. Rapidly, she opened one drawer after another. She looked under the bed and even opened up Ulrike's suitcase. But then she was interrupted.

She heard the key turn in the front door and voices entering the house. Hastily, she smoothed everything back into place and clambered down the ladder. Then she slipped silently into her bedroom to gather her thoughts, while below she could hear Kiki, Durga and Ulrike chattering in the kitchen.

She turned towards her dressing table. She almost dreaded checking her things. She didn't want to find anything else missing.

That was when she saw the note. It was propped up in front of the mirror and wedged with one of her lipsticks.

'Dear Mum and Dad . . .' She read it through

with amazement. When she had finished, she went racing downstairs calling out, 'Ulrike! Anil! Where are you? Come here, everyone!'

Ulrike and Kiki immediately appeared in the hallway. Mrs Dalal rushed up and clasped Kiki in her arms. Looking at Ulrike, she almost burst into tears.

'Ulrike! Where's Anil?'

'He hasn't come home yet,' replied Ulrike, puzzled by the mother's emotion.

'Shouldn't he be back now? Isn't he usually here at the same time as you?' cried Mother desperately.

'Yes, he is . . . we were just beginning to wonder where he could be,' said Ulrike. 'Shall I go to the school and look for him?'

'What's the matter, Mum?' asked Kiki, studying her mother's worried face. 'Is anything wrong?'

'No! Yes! Not really . . . Oh, I don't know!' wailed Mother. 'Oh Kiki, did you realise that Anil had been taking things – stealing from me?'

Kiki gasped in astonishment, and her mother realised that she didn't know.

Mrs Dalal could hardly bring herself to look at Ulrike, so ashamed did she feel, but she said in a whisper, 'Forgive me, Ulrike, for a while, I suspected you. So many things of mine have gone missing, I never dreamed it was Anil, but look!' She held out the note. 'I think he's run away!'

They forgot about Durga. Mother, Ulrike and Kiki rushed into the car and drove off to the school to search for Anil. Durga walked out into the garden and stood in the middle of the lawn. She stood with her legs apart and arms outstretched, and her face tipped upwards to the sky.

There was a faint quivering of leaves; somewhere, a blackbird burst out singing and the fox, crouching in the undergrowth, looked at Durga through narrowed eyes.

Anil was running. He'd been on the run all day, and finally he had found his way back to the park where the chase started. He was running, running, running; thrashing through the bushes, darting round trees, tumbling into hollows and ditches, desperately looking for a hiding place, a haven, a place of safety; somewhere where his enemies couldn't find him, not now, not ever.

But this was no jungle which could swallow up a person forever. This was just a city park, where no undergrowth lasted very long, and every now and then it gave way to neat open flower beds, or an ornamental lake, or tennis courts or a putting green. Where could he go?

Suddenly the three boys broke into view. They saw him and waved their arms threateningly. Anil's chest was beginning to hurt. He wondered if he could take another breath into his exhausted lungs. Before him were the wide open playing fields; nowhere to hide there, but he stumbled towards them because there was nowhere else to go.

'We've got him now!' laughed Goutam. Anil was limping with fatigue. The three boys were closing in on him fast.

Now they were only a few metres away. The boys stopped running and just stood there triumphantly, with their arms folded before them. He wouldn't run any more. Anil had flopped into an exhausted heap.

They began to advance, slowly. Then, suddenly,

they halted in their tracks. They could hear a strange noise. It was a steady rustling in the undergrowth, even though there were no shrubs or bushes, only the short, bleak grass of the windswept playing fields. But it was as if they were in a jungle, and could hear some great creature padding towards them.

'Crruck . . . crruck . . . crruck.' It wasn't a loud noise. Not even as loud as someone prowling secretly through the bushes. It was as soft as rain falling on dry leaves, yet it had a terrifying weight to it. This was no prowling cat or sniffing dog . . . This was . . .

Goutam, Ricky and Carl gasped in horror, as a huge, powerful, golden shape sprang into view; it came wheeling round as if sizing up its prey, cutting off their line of escape as the boys broke into a panic-stricken run.

Anil, crouching with his head in his hands, looked up. Durga! She couldn't be there in reality, for she rode on a lion; ten arms whirled about her head, and from the middle of her forehead, a third eye burned like a fiery furnace. She was a fearful sight.

144

The lion stopped and crouched low to the ground; all its muscles flexed, poised and ready to strike. It gathered itself back on its giant haunches, and then, with a dreadful roar, launched itself into the air.

There was a sound of screaming. The boys were screaming, Anil was screaming. Anil felt the hot breath of the lion searing his face, he saw the white jagged tips of its teeth and its long red tongue. Then Durga's ten arms seemed to gather him up; it was like being snatched into a whirlpool and swept along. Was he living, dying, flying or plunging? Then he realised he was sitting; he was sitting with Durga on the lion's back as if he were a king or a god.

Far below him, he saw Goutam, Ricky and Carl running like rabbits.

There's something terrible about being found out; when suddenly everyone knows exactly what you are; when people realise that you're not as clever as they thought, as brave as they thought or as powerful and strong as they thought.

'Where are we going?' he asked in a small voice.

'Home,' answered Durga.

'No,' said Anil, suddenly defiant. 'I can't go home yet. Not like this.'

Then the earth was rushing towards him. The trees and the playing fields tipped and spun, as though a giant hand twirled the globe on its axis.

Anil slid from the lion's back and stood at the park gates, blocking the exit. His tormentors came stumbling towards him. They stopped dead in their tracks. They trembled in amazement. Was this the boy they had teased and tormented? Anil looked taller, broader, as powerful as a lion, and, most terrifying of all, there smouldered in the middle of his forehead, an eye like the cavern of a volcano, which they didn't dare look at for more than a split second, in case it burned them up.

They bowed their heads like cowards and fled.

The fox stood in the night garden looking up at the window of the smallest spare bedroom at the back of the house. The curtains were not drawn, because the person who had been sleeping there had now gone.

The garden, the trees, the moon and the fox

146

had all made their farewells to Durga.

Everyone was asleep; Mother and Father, contented with their lot; Ulrike, up in her loft; Kiki was sleeping with a little smile on her face because she had been invited out to tea. Above her bed on the wall was the poster of the goddess riding a lion, which Durga had given her.

Only Anil was not asleep. He stood at his bedroom window. He saw the fox and they stared at each other. Suddenly, a vast shadow emerged out of the undergrowth. It glistened like gold in the silvery light; its great muscles and sinews rippled as it walked slowly across the lawn. The lion paused only for a second to look up at Anil with its burning eyes, before it gave a great leap, up, up, up into the starry night sky and disappeared over the roof of the house.

Anil would have told everyone about it the next morning, only he forgot.

Glossary

Agni   God of Fire

bhaji   vegetable doughnut

Brahma   God of Creation

Diwali   Festival of Light

drone   a single note played in the background of
a piece of music

dupatta   veil, part of Indian dress

Durga   Goddess of Peace and Friendship

guru   a teacher

Hanuman   Monkey God

henna   a brown/orange plant dye

Himalayas   mountain range in central Asia

Kali   Goddess of Destruction

kofti   meatball

Lakshmi/Sita   Goddess of Wealth and Prosperity

naan   type of bread

namaste   greeting

Narakasura   God of Darkness

pakoras   type of savoury

poories   type of bread

Rama   Vishnu on earth

rangoli   pattern

Ravana   God of Demons

saree   Indian dress

salvar kameez   Indian tunic and pyjamas

samosas   pastry triangles containing vegetables
       or meat

Sita   Lakshmi on earth

Shiva   Lord Shiva, the Destroyer of Evil, and
       husband of Kali

tabla   pairs of drums used in traditional Indian
       music

tanpura   a stringed instrument used in
       traditional Indian music

tilak   a dot worn by Hindus on their foreheads.
       It is a sign of welcome and wisdom

Varun   God of Water

Vayu   God of Wind

veena   stringed musical instrument

Vishnu   Preserver of Creation